Dangerou

Tracey-Anne Forbes

Dangerous Places

The characters and events in this story are fictitious and any resemblance to
real people is purely coincidental.

Dangerous Places
ISBN 978 1 76109 182 7
Copyright © Tracey-Anne Forbes 2021
Cover photo by Tracey-Anne Forbes of a partial image of *Jupiter et Encelade*
by Anne and Patrick Poirier

First published 2021 by
GINNINDERRA PRESS
PO Box 3461 Port Adelaide 5015
www.ginninderrapress.com.au

'I feel so strange, as if I were living in a myth –'
'Myths are dangerous places.'
'But we are safe, aren't we, aren't we, my dear, dear one?'

Iris Murdoch, *The Green Knight*

There are only the pursued, the pursuing, the busy, and the tired.

F. Scott Fitzgerald, *The Great Gatsby*

1

It's a house from a dream, I think. I stop the car, which shudders as if shrugging off the rain. The children are asleep, strapped up snugly, so I sit for a moment in the quiet, falling rain and look down at the house. It seems to crouch on the very edge of a cliff; in front of it are only steel-silver sea and a ribbon of surf, breaking on a sandbank far out. It's at the bottom of a hill, embedded in and overhung by a pool of sluggish, rain-sodden foliage. I can't even see what colour the walls are painted – only a rain-sheened tin roof with choked gutters. No wonder, with all those gums, I think. Trust Peri to live in such an impractical place. The rain keeps running down the car window, obscuring my view. There is no driveway: Peri's green Honda is parked in front of me.

I wake Ross, who stammers from dreams to excitement. 'Are we here? We're here! Sharlie, wake up! Come on, little darling! We're at the beach! Where's your pony?'

He often mixes my phrases with his own as he wakes. He loves waking up – or being awake, to be more precise. Sharlie loves sleeping, and cuddling sleepily, and thoughtful, imaginative games involving names of her toys or the friends Ross makes.

We pull on raincoats, and Ross drags out his fishing rod and tackle box, and I take only their beach bags and carry Sharlie, who clutches her pony and nestles her yellow-hooded head into my shoulder. We climb down broad, slippery stone steps, which wind like a ski trail through the thicket. Ross forges ahead, thrashing a path with a broken stick and his rod, and chattering excitedly. It seems to go on and on – and then suddenly the house is before us.

Even Ross is quiet then. It is dark – we are well under the canopy – and the house, olive-green weatherboard, emerges only dimly. Palms, sugar gums, bottlebrush and jacarandas drip and trail their leaves possessively over the path to it. It rests on short timber stumps; there are three or four new, freshly painted steps up to a roofed veranda. The front door, inset with a pane of bumpy, lead-light glass, is flanked by eight-paned windows. Leaves are reflected in the lead-crazed glass of the door and on the smooth, glazed window glass, and the leaves flicker on the glass so it winks like teary eyes. Rain beads and drips from the gutters of the roof. Honeysuckle twists its green filigree around the house stumps and up to the veranda floor.

There is a knocker on the door. I bang it, heartily, because Ross's hand has crept into the crook of the arm in which I still cradle Sharlie. The paint on the house itself, I notice, is flaking, showing smudges of a previous paler green.

After a moment, we hear footsteps and then the door opens.

'Ven! Venny! God, what a terrible weekend for – oh, it's good to see you!' She draws the door fully open and throws out her arms.

We clash noses kissing.

'You too – how long has it been? Six months?' I breathe in her scent of a perfume I'd forgotten. Dressed in an oversized pullover and long hippie skirt, her body feels small and fragile, but graceful, as a cat's can when it jumps into your lap.

'More – or it feels like it. Escaped – I have escaped! But – Rossy – little Ross – you haven't forgotten me?' She bends to him, but he ducks his face behind Sharlie, pulling heavily on my arm. She laughs. 'Okay, I won't kiss you. And Charlotte – this is Charlotte? This little face, all shy too? Oh God, Venny, they've grown – and you look so well –'

I stand smiling, taking her hand with my free one. 'And you're much too thin!' I say.

Because she has lost weight – lost a roundness she used to have. But it's not just that: she looks changed, somehow. It's not her hair, even though that's longer than I remember and gathered in a black fountain cascading from the top of her head; nor the black eyeliner she has around her eyes or the pieces of shell which swing and clatter from her neck to between her breasts: all of these reflect a style she has had since she was a teenager. It's something less concrete – a sort of electricity, nervous, contagious – a pent-up excitement, or anticipation. She's my cousin, two years younger than me, and I've known her all my life, so I know it's not just my imagination.

'Living on the island must be agreeing with you. Or is it all these steps you have to climb to get out of the place? It's like nothing I've ever seen.' I turn from her to look back up, but the foliage is so thick I can barely see the sodden sky.

She laughs a piping, gurgling laugh – the notes dipping and peaking like birdsong. 'Beggars can't be choosers. Not too many places here you can caretake for nothing with views like this one has. Come on – come in and see. We'll get the rest of your stuff when it stops raining.'

We trail after her graceful, loose figure, past closed doors, along an unlit corridor, dark even after the grey light outside. The rain is very quiet on the roof, like a quietly burning fire. There is a smell of dust and old carpet, and the air is so cold it might have been refrigerated.

'That's my room there.' Her arm gestures vaguely to the left, to an open doorway.

As I pass it, I glimpse partially drawn, thick curtains, a heavy oak bed and a white swath of mosquito net. Then the corridor right-angles and I can make out stair banisters ahead. We follow her down, in just enough light to make out our path.

'What is this? The bowels of the earth?' My voice echoes hollowly; I have no idea how far ahead of us she is. Ross's grip and Sharlie's weight are burning my arm.

'Keep coming!'

Then suddenly there is a flush of light: a grey rectangle of daylight in which dust motes drift; Peri has opened a door at the bottom of the stairs. We pass through it and emerge in a room on the edge of the cliff.

'Wow.'

Ross loosens his grip on my arm, and stares too. For the room we've entered seems to float above a view from a glass wall overlooking the sea.

'Wow,' I say again. I move slowly, still carrying Sharlie, with Ross over to the glass – a series of floor-deep, timber-framed windows with French doors at their end, leading out to a deck and steps.

'Yes.' Peri's voice is excited, a little triumphant. 'Pretty spectacular, isn't it?'

For it is: grey waves crashing and breaking on a sandbar far out, then heaving laced violence at the cliff foot below us; rain pelting mist in moving swaths above the waves so that sea and air become one.

'You're not kidding.'

'I just couldn't believe my luck. Haden, the guy who owns it – got that glass put in as soon as he bought the place, apparently – it's just the best thing – you never get tired of that view, of looking at the sea – it's always changing, always different. So, so different from Proserpine!' She's shaking her head and smiling. 'Hasn't done much else since then, mind you – too busy, I guess. He's some VIP in the mines over here, and has houses all over the place. Buys, renovates, sells. Has heaps of dough.'

I drag my eyes from the view to look back at the rest of the room. It's large and open, running the full width of the house – a dining room, lounge room and kitchen in one. At the far end, the kitchen is divided from the other areas by a laminated bar. The picture-glass wall clashes startlingly with the other walls, which are painted a dingy brown, and it sits oddly against the floor ,which is carpeted in a thin nylon whose pile has worn through in places. But Peri's things, the things I recognise as in her taste, complement the room's simplicity and quality beautifully: long, comfortable sofas; her pottery displayed around the shelves and some of her paintings on the walls; her crystals suspended from the ceiling to catch the light; her ornamental lamps.

'Well, you've made it look great anyhow. How long's he had it?'

Peri shrugs. 'Not sure. But he doesn't want to let it, apparently – just wants someone here to keep an eye on it. Till he can finish fixing it up, probably. I was just so lucky. Met him the first day I came over here – he nearly collected me with his car. Then he was really apologetic

– took me to a doctor 'cause I landed on the road and bumped my head. Think he must have had the guilts about the whole thing and that's why he offered this place to me when the other one fell through.'

Sharlie suddenly wriggles, and I move over to one of the couches and drop her onto it, then help her out of her raincoat.

I straighten, and rub my forearm. 'Ugh – she's getting heavy!' I take off my own coat and flip my hair from its heavy chignon and comb it with my fingers so it falls warmly around my shoulders to my waist like a sort of cape.

Peri's moved over behind the laminated bar. 'Now, what do you feel like? Something to eat? Or a drink?' She opens a cupboard and pulls out a bottle of whisky: she tips it at me, one eyebrow raised.

I hesitate. It's a bit early...but I'm on my own, I don't have to drive anywhere, and she's already unscrewing the cap. 'Lovely.'

I move over to a kitchen barstool, and Sharlie follows, clinging to my jeans. I lift her onto my lap. Ross stays at the window, looking out.

'What would you like, Sharl? Juice? And are you hungry?' Peri has her head on one side, smiling.

Sharlie nods, wordlessly.

'God, she's so blonde. You guys are so lucky. Brown skin, blue eyes, blond hair – it's not fair. The rest of us are such bloody wogs. How you managed it is beyond me.' She's emptying potato straws and salted cashews into shell-shaped bowls.

'Grandpa was blond, remember? Before he was grey? The northern Italian Gran met during the war. Remember her telling us that story when we were little? And Mark was quite fair when he was younger.'

'Don't care. It's still not fair.' She picks up her glass and holds it to mine. We clink.

'All's fair in love and war – and genetics.' I sip the whisky. 'Mmm – that's nice. Settle my stomach. The trip over was a bit rough, wasn't it, Rossy?'

'Mmm.' He's come over behind me, eyeing the food sideways around me. 'Can we go to the beach soon, Mum?'

'Well, it's raining a bit at the moment. We saw lots of jellyfish from the ferry, didn't we, guys?'

'Huge ones.' Sharlie suddenly becomes animated, her eyes as big as her imagination. 'As big as this.' She holds her arms wide, her little, heart-shaped face framed angelically by her fair fall of hair – then drops her arms quickly. She hides her head in my shoulder.

'Not that big.' Ross's voice is reproving – echoing his father's – but his concentration is on the potato straws.

'What'll you have, Ross? Juice? Or what about hot chocolate?'

I see both my children light up. 'Okay,' I sigh, 'this once. Thanks, Peri. I've brought over a few things, but they're still in the car.'

'No problem.' She microwaves milk in the oven I recognise as hers too, and, with a wink at Ross, spoons in far more chocolate than I ever would.

Ross climbs onto a stool, temporarily pacified.

'So,' I say when she's finally settled with her own drink, 'the big escape, huh?'

She rolls her eyes and silver bangles on her wrist clash as she flicks hair from her face. 'Well, it's a start. Wasn't really planned, you know. Came over for a holiday after first term of that Ag. Science course I was doing at Gatton, and just – stayed. Met some people – stayed in spare rooms for a while – and then this place came up three weeks ago. And there's this guy.' She lifts her glass and grins, looking as me sideways.

I grin back. 'Thought there might be.'

'Ven, he is just…uuhh! Nothing's happened yet, but…'

'It won't be long before it does?'

'That's what I'm hoping!' Her brown eyes glitter.

I sip my drink, looking at her. Then I say, 'I'm glad, Peri. Really glad. Glad you got away, more than anything. Much as I like Aunt Demi. But she's got to let you go, eventually. You are twenty-eight, after all. And she's got plenty of people to help her with the farm these days. Even Mum's on your side.'

'Ah! So you've been discussing me.'

'Well, your mum rang – she was worried cause you hadn't contacted her – thought you might be in trouble, et cetera, et cetera. So when you invited me over, of course they all jumped on me...'

'To come and spy?' She's suddenly frowning, looking cross.

'No!'

'Ven, I can't contact her. Not yet. She'll talk me into going back – give me the guilts. The trip about everything being left to me and how I have responsibilities – how hard she's worked since Dad died, how if I finished my Ag. Science degree I'd be such a help, how she'd trusted me to finish it down here instead of externally...'

I rub the wet strands of hair on my forehead: I can feel I'm frowning too. 'Yes, yes, I know, Peri. I didn't come over to spy on you for them – really! Certainly not to talk you into going back. I came because you invited me and I wanted to see you and I needed a break too –'

'From Mark?' Her eyes are suddenly interested.

I grimace, glancing at the children. She gets the hint. 'Just from home. Need a holiday. Don't we, guys?'

Ross and Sharlie have been quietly eating, waging a silent competition for proximity to Peri's bowls. Sharlie has wriggled gradually to the edge of my knee.

Now Ross looks up, his eyes the vivid blue that first attracted me to their father. He glances at the glass wall. 'Hey,' he says, 'it's stopped raining. Can we go to the beach now?'

Peri seems as relieved as I am to drop the subject of her mother. 'Don't see why not! Did you bring your buckets and spades?'

'Sure!'

Sharlie doesn't speak, but the expression in her eyes exactly mimics Ross's.

'We've got all sorts of shapes – circles and stars, hearts – and I brought my fishing line. Can I go fishing Mum? Please? Please?'

'What, after you've dug up all those poor worms this morning, you think I won't let you use them?' I say, rubbing his head.

There are steps cut into the cliff and an iron handrail running beside them. They lead steeply down to a sheltered cove, sandy, protected on both sides by outcrops of rock. Ross leads the way, jiggling his buckets and fishing line and tackle. He's changed into his swimmers but at my insistence is still wearing a sweater. Peri carries towels and a picnic basket with hats and drinks and glasses. I hold Charlotte's hand and we move slowly in the rear of the procession.

Peri and I settle on the strip of rain-pitted sand from which the high tide has withdrawn. Ross climbs off deftly among rocks jutting into the sea, with his line and jar of bait. Charlotte begins to search around for beach treasures: she bends from the hip, with her bare legs bowed straight as a ballerina's; and with her fair fine hair and loose, long jumper I'm reminded of the changeling child I always thought she was when she was younger. The late afternoon sun slants obliquely through a gap in clearing cloud, as strange and beautiful as an illustration from child-hood mythology.

For a while, Peri and I lie silently on our towels, glasses of whisky and soda wedged in the sand. I still feel a bit awkward about our conversation about her mother: her guilt was so strong I could almost feel it emanating from her skin back in the house. Her bond with her mother is so, so powerful – I know that – she's the only child, a long-awaited one at that; and no child could have been more dearly loved. It must have taken a lot of courage for her to take this step. A lot of courage to virtually say to her mother, maybe other people are going to be as important to me as you are.

Well, I think, maybe this man she's met will be the answer to her problems. Maybe he'll be the one to change her life. Because my gut feeling is that unless she does bond strongly with someone else, her mother will eventually get her back.

It is almost warm. A pile of Charlotte's treasure grows between Peri and me: scraps of seaweed, sour-smelling and shredded like tobacco; chunks of knobby coral, pitted with holes like old bone; dried, russet leaves curled into tiny gondolas; palm fronds flaky and fragile but still intact; green, pumpkin-shaped seeds the size of walnuts; driftwood hollowed and sucked by the sea to the consistency of cork; a shaggy, battered coconut.

The whisky is mellow and makes the light sharp and my heart warm, and I suddenly don't feel like thinking about Peri's problems any more. I have come over here for my own reasons as well, to escape my own problems. I close my eyes and sniff.

The seaweed reeks of nostalgia. On this island, I met Yanni. Yanni. Unguarded, I am suffused with a memory – then immediately guilt. No, scolds my chiding mother-heart: you came here with Mark too…

Mark. Yes. On our honeymoon. To this island. When I was twenty-four and Mark thirty-two. Not to this secluded, barren, northern side, but back to the west, where the surf is not so violent and there are sleepy townships and jetties used more for fishing than anything else. I brought him: to a house called 'Serenity'; and in it I made him serene. The beach was fifty metres from the house and all the old cabins in front of it were empty or washed away, and only my grandmother's ancient friend was still living next door, in her shadowed memories of the old days; and we floated in the green glass sea and he chipped oysters from the boulders placed to ward off the channel and we swallowed the oysters while we floated, his hard body rocking warmly beneath my weight, my haltered breasts drifting on the black hair of his wet chest, the oysters tangy as lemon and creamy as taramasalata and my excitement so urgent I had to close my eyes and –

'How are you and Mark going anyway?' Peri rolls onto her back and looks up at me as if she has read my thoughts. Her eyes are as translucent as amber, and the afternoon sun honeys her calmed face.

I grimace. The image of his face, the face he turns so often to me now, flashes unbidden in my memory: eyes stony, grey as a winter sky, untouchable, lips pressed thinly together above his grey-streaked beard.

'Oh. You know what he's like. Moody. Workaholic. And he does make beautiful things. And he's always been like that, I know – it's just that lately he's…oh, I don't want to talk about it.' Compared to that earlier memory. 'Later, okay?'

She smiles. 'Not in front of the children. Oh, it's good having you here! What shall we do tonight? Let's have fish and chips and salad and some of that wine you brought. Get the children to bed and play some old music. Solve the problems of the universe? And tomorrow the beach again and maybe lunch at the pub. You never know – you might decide not to ever leave either!' She sits up and reaches for the picnic basket, grinning cheekily.

2

When the breeze comes up and our shadows lie like slender ghosts on the sand, we pack up and go back to the house. I bath the children then leave them temporarily in their day clothes helping Peri in the kitchen while I go up to the car to collect the rest of our things. The whiskies have given me energy – and courage. Why I need courage is questionable: but I find myself shrinking from that upper, black void of the house we passed through on the way to the cliff room. The fear is insubstantial: of old fears of the dark; of a vague terror of the unknown; of the stale, dusty smell of a past transported to the present.

Peri has told me the corridor light has blown and she has lent me a torch; I feel my way cautiously through the blackness, up steps, past doors I can see in the torchlight are tall and blackened with age. It's an expensive house, I can't help thinking, despite my jumpiness. Run-down, but probably beautiful in its time. And could be again, with the right handling. It occurs to me that Peri would have the ability to restore it, not to a former glory, but to a unique, shimmering, fresh beauty, to a style blending its flavours of heritage with its position on the edge of both the earth and the sea: its essential grandeur with its sandy, salt-sprayed, holiday languor. It would be something she would love to do – something which could draw on her artistic and imaginative talents – talents her mother has never recognised or nurtured. Then I shake myself. The house has nothing to do with her, really – she's just care-taking it. And she's in love with someone else on the island, not this Haden, who doesn't seem particularly interested in renovating it in a hurry anyway.

The reflected torch beam gleams on the coloured glass in the front door then, and I pass through it and climb up the winding path to the car. I gather our things, lock the car and reverse the journey awkwardly.

Peri is serving up dinner when I get back. She has a cassette on and an artist I don't recognise is singing a throaty, heart-wrenching song and Peri has opened a bottle of Chardonnay and is dancing around the kitchen, her black hair flaring out from its topknot, her skirt swinging and flipping against her legs. I dump the bags on a couch, and feel suddenly happy, just looking at her.

We eat poached fish and singed chips and a crispy salad. None of us mind the burnt chips; we all eat them anyway.

'That must be one of the biggest pluses of living here: a never-ending supply of fresh fish,' I say between mouthfuls. I am hungry and a bit drunk: we've nearly finished the bottle of Chardonnay.

'Mmm. And you can get it for a song, if you know the right people. Or catch it yourself. You didn't have much luck this afternoon, Rossy, 'cause the tide wasn't right. But you can catch fish off those rocks if you know what you're doing. I'll have to show you: maybe tomorrow?' Peri places a forkful of fish on a lettuce leaf and rolls it to munch.

'Tomorrow morning – early?' Ross's eyes are bright with hope.

'Peri might want to sleep in,' I interrupt gently. I don't want Peri to get Ross's hopes up: he's not used to disappointment, and I know Peri – her favourite waking time is definitely not early.

'I'll have to look up the tides,' says Peri, glancing at me. 'Your mum's got a point there.'

'We'll work something out,' I say quickly. 'Now, are you both finished?'

'Mmm. That was yum,' says Charlotte, climbing onto my lap. 'Can I have my dessert now, Mummy?'

'What would you like?' Peri begins to stack the plates.

'Ice cream.'

'Please,' I say.

'Ple-ase!'

'I think we can manage that,' says Peri, winking at me.

I've brought over their favourite: made with real strawberries and cream.

'And after that, teeth, toilet, bed, okay?'

'Okay!' Charlotte has already scampered after Peri and Ross to the refrigerator.

Peri takes us to a room down a corridor from the cliff room. It's in a wing on the eastern side of the house, perpendicular to the sea. 'I think this must have been converted at some stage to some sort of holiday guest house,' Peri says, flicking on lights and opening windows. 'This room's been tacked on – with a modern bathroom to boot. Thought you'd rather be down here than up in one of those dusty little bedrooms upstairs.'

I think again of the dark, heavy feel of the upper house, and shiver slightly. 'Thanks – this is great. But why don't you sleep down here?'

Peri shrugs and smiles. 'Dunno. Quite like the room I'm in. Has a sort of strange, unearthly feel. I've done heaps of sketches of it – trying to capture its mood. Hoping it'll somehow permeate me if I sleep there long enough.'

I stop my unpacking of toothbrushes momentarily and glance at her. 'Is it the main bedroom?'

'Mmm.' She's straightening the counterpane of the trundle bed made up on the floor for Ross.

I watch her curiously, but she doesn't look up or say anything more. Again, I wonder about this Haden who owns the place, and about Peri's relationship with him. Why has she gone to so much effort to make the place liveable, and why does she sleep in his bedroom? Surely a caretaker wouldn't normally do that?

But she obviously seems to feel no further explanation is needed: she's straightened and is helping me unpack the children's things. So I dismiss it as well. It's perhaps just the way she does things.

After I've read the children a story, I tuck Charlotte into the double bed she is to share with me, and Ross into his trundle. The sheets smell of fresh washing and a little of salt. Even Charlotte has eaten properly, and both the children's bellies are heavy with potatoes and fish and ice cream. I kiss them tenderly, turn on a lamp, and leave them to sleep.

Peri has cleaned up the kitchen when I return to her, and is lying on the long Genoa, listening to the end of a Bruce Springsteen song. Her buoyant mood seems to have quietened with the music. 'My home town,' Springsteen sings, his voice full of sadness; 'm-y home town'. There is another opened bottle of Chardonnay on the coffee table. Some of the deep windows are open – they unclip, I see, and hinge partially open like casement windows – and air as cold as water washes in. The sky has cleared, the clouds swept like distractions out of sight.

Peri lies on her front in her oversized blue pullover with her chin digging into her hands on the armrest. With her black, cascading hair and careless skirt, she looks suddenly young and vulnerable. I pour myself a glass of wine and sit down quietly and we both listen to the song and stare out at the cold white stars.

'It's really beautiful,' I say in the silence of the finished CD, 'just beautiful here.'

'Yes. Yes it is. I just love it, love this house…'

'It must be so peaceful, so different a world.'

'Mmm. So different, yes. You know, sometimes it's hard to imagine Proserpine; isn't that strange? I lived there for so long, and now I seem hardly to remember it. Home. School. The town itself.' Her voice is distant and a little lost.

'Maybe you don't really want to.'

'Mmm, you could be right.'

We are silent for a moment: I know she's thinking of her mother. But I don't want to get onto that subject again, so I say quickly, brightly, 'Well, tell me about this guy you've met. What he's like, what his name is…'

She rolls over then onto her side, and props her head on an elbow. Her eyes are suddenly alight, not misty and reflective any more, and her earlier animation returns. Then there is a moment, just a moment, when she takes a breath and goes to speak, then doesn't, then takes another breath, and then she says, 'Oh, Venny, but you know him. You used to know him, a long time ago – we both did – remember that time I came to Amity for a holiday with you…'

I'm staring at her – from the moment she hesitated, I've been freezing, slowly freezing, all my reflexes paralysing, all my nerves still, quite still.

'Yanni. You remember him? There's only one Yanni.' She's looking at me, a smile beginning to break open, her face lighting up, a little catch in her last word as she says his name a second time, her hand automatically reaching for the wineglass on the carpet beside her couch, for the wine which hasn't been the trigger to lift her spirits but which she searches out nevertheless –

I can't move. I am afraid to speak.

'He's back here. On the island. He asked about you.'

Wine roars, then, suddenly, in my head. Or my blood. I am full of frightening wine – or frightening possibility. I sit quite, quite still. Breathe, I think, breathe. Then I whisper, 'He can't be. He was in Sydney –'

'Was. He's back here now. Got a surf shop, brings stuff up from down south.' She's looking at me, the radiant smile changing slowly, a small frown of concern starting. She lifts the wineglass to her mouth.

I watch her hand, with its long and pale pink fingernails – fingernails which have always been a hallmark of hers, despite the farm, despite hard, rough work on her mother's farm – and the hand looks suddenly unfamiliar, incongruous, like a series of notes from one song suddenly played in the middle of another.

I can't ask her anything more. I want to say, is he flirting with you? Is he seducing you? Has he taken you to the cave, our cave? But I can't bear to know. I can't bear to think about it.

'Venny? Are you okay?' She's sitting up, leaning forward, frowning, curious, still holding the glass. 'How did you know he went to Sydney?'

I blink and look down and lift my own glass and quickly sip. 'Oh, well, you know – he was good friends with Luke. And me too, really. We were close, sort of – always saw him on holidays. There weren't too many kids to play with at Amity, and he did live practically next door. Luke and I followed his career a bit. He was such a good surfer.' My voice has dropped to almost a mumble. I raise it, and my eyes. 'But I haven't seen him for so, so long.'

Not for eleven years. Not since that day, that morning, when he came to see me and he took me fiercely and he held me and stroked me afterwards, stroking my hair down my side as he might a cat, absently; and he told me that he was leaving. That he was leaving the island, leaving Queensland: that he had to experience life. But that he would come back, he would come back to me when he was ready. And I nodded, dumbly. I understood, of course I understood. We had talked of it before – the need for him to stretch his wings, expand his horizons, all the clichés...

But he never came back. And all I could think later, much later, was that men mustn't love the way women do, wholly, unconditionally, with every part of their consciousness and unconsciousness...the way I loved Yanni.

I grimace. 'Sorry. It was just a bit of a surprise, that's all. I mean – from what I remember, you didn't seem particularly interested in him when you came over for that holiday.'

She looks at me over the rim of her glass, pressing its bulb against her lips, her eyes large and very dark brown. 'Well, I thought he was – a bit full of himself.'

Yes. He had been that. I'd teased him about it, playfully, once: and he'd grinned his infectious grin at me and told me I was the only one on the island who deserved him. So I shouldn't complain.

'So he isn't any longer?'

A smile spreads slowly and dreamily across her face again then; she lowers the glass. 'Maybe a bit. But I don't mind it so much any more.'

I can't bear it. I can't bear the expression she has on her face – dreamy, hopeful, in love with him – I stand up abruptly, still holding my glass, and cross to the open windows. 'Did you hear a car? I thought I heard a car slowing.' Of course I can't see anything except the black-glinting sea – and what I heard was probably only the hush of a withdrawing wave – but it's enough of an excuse to be distracted, to move.

'Are you expecting anyone? It's such a deserted... I'm not sure if I locked the car properly...'

'Oh, it'll be safe.' Peri's voice is smiling. 'You're not in a city here, remember! No one can steal a car and get away with it on this island. I never lock mine.' She suddenly yawns, even her stretch audible. 'And no, I'm not expecting anyone. Worse luck.'

I turn around then, leaning my back against a window frame. 'So tell me,' I say, forcing my voice and body to relax, 'about the rest of the people you've met over here.' I try a smile, and go back over to the couch.

It is only later, when I am warmly under the feather duvet beside Charlotte, that I allow myself to think about Yanni again. He asked about me. Yes, while he was flirting with Peri. He might, after all this time, have come back to keep his promise. Like hell. Like hell. Promises you make when you are seventeen mean as little as wishes on stars. If I can see him, just see him once alone, he might tell me why he has never returned to me. Sure. Like he'd remember. Like he'd remember why he dumped a stupid, lovesick bitch more than a decade ago.

He's still single.

I'm not.

I close my eyes. All I can hear is the sea breaking and withdrawing on the little cove beach and on the ridges of rocks which run out from it and, very distantly, on a sandbank far out.

Oh, what does it matter? I think. Even if, even if we met, we talked alone, he wanted to... No, I think. No. Nothing could come of it.

Because I have borne children. Adorable, slave-driving, autocratic children, who love both me and their father and need us both; whom I love more, much more than any man, more than myself.

Fuck him, I think. Fuck Yanni. I don't want to see him.

And that's what keeps running through my sleep as the sea sweeps beneath my consciousness and a blank-faced moon casts dark and cloud-swept shadows in the alien bedroom whenever I stir.

Fucking him.

3

At eight the next morning, I awake with a start. The house is quiet and the bedroom cool. The children are still asleep, unusually; perhaps because we are all in the one bed, Ross having come in with Charlotte and me during the night. We are all snuggled up warmly together under a feather duvet. Sunlight from the northern windows angles across my feet. Not raining, then.

I have woken from a dream of Yanni. In the dream, we were lying together on the sundeck of an ocean liner. We didn't touch each other, but he was so close I could feel the heat from his skin. We talked about Greece, which was where we were going on the boat, and then we talked about marriage. I was with an old boyfriend, Richard, on the boat, and Yanni thought I was to marry Richard. I told him I never would marry anyone, because the man I loved had long left me.

Suddenly the ship was sinking. Yanni and I were washed overboard and dragged under by the pull of the drowning boat. We were caught, however, by a net, but realised there was another net underneath the one we were on that had been cast earlier to catch passengers. The passengers, and incidental sea life, were all drowning; but Yanni and I were okay, on top of our net, and breathing freely.

It is an easy dream for me to interpret. I have become good at interpreting the dreams I have of Yanni. I have dreamed of him regularly, on and off, for as long as I have been an adult; even at times when he has had no conscious place in my thoughts.

I creep quietly from the bed and the floor is cold on my bare feet. I wash in the adjoining bathroom with the door shut, but by the time I emerge both the children are awake. Ross wants immediately to go fishing, and we argue about it in loud whispers until he accepts reluctantly my promise of 'this afternoon'. Then they take it in turns to run across the cold floor to the bathroom and back to bed. We read some stories they have brought with them; after, while they dress, I make tea and toast. Surprisingly, I have not a trace of a hangover: perhaps because we've slept so late.

There is still no sound from Peri even after I've cleaned up, so I leave a note for her on the kitchen bench. She was always a notoriously late riser on holidays we spent together: perhaps in passive rebellion against the sunrising hours her mother expected her to keep when work on their sugar cane farm was intense. I pack a beach bag, and I unlock the French doors leading out to the deck; Ross runs ahead to search out a track up the side of the house and Sharlie and I follow him along it and then up the winding, dappled path to the car.

I drive to Amity Harbour. I park the car in the curved driveway of Serenity, a silent, lopsided house bordering the sea.

The house belongs to my paternal grandmother. For thirty years, she and my grandfather lived here; then in their retirement they abandoned it more and more, travelling to Asia and around Australia. Whenever they were away, they left the house to my father and his children to use while they were gone. I was the only one of the grandchildren who used it, though. Later, my grandfather became sick and they returned here; then he died. My grandmother is still alive, but my father's sister has shifted her to Brisbane, into a flat where she can keep an eye on her. My grandmother insisted on seeing the shift as a temporary one, though, and took only essentials with her. The house is still as she left it, filled with her and my dead grandfather's lives; and I have keys to it.

I haven't been here since my honeymoon: not to Amity, not to this house. Somehow it seemed too far, too much of an effort with all the paraphernalia of babies, then too much for my grandmother to cope with, and too dangerous to growing children with the sea so close.

I walk in bare feet up the sandy, poinciana-roofed path to the house, a child's hand in each of mine. The path reeks of memory. The smell of paperbarks and giant staghorns – the splintery feel on my feet of debris in the sand – the sound of crickets or cicadas in the morning sun – all these things are memories as old as childhood to me.

I take the enamel cup from its hook beside the rainwater tank tap and pour a drink, from habit. It tastes rusty, as I remember. I unlock the sliding glass door. The first things I notice, as I always have, are my father's paintings lining the walls. Oils of old boots and jackets, of a young Grandpa and Grandma, of fishing boats, of jetties, of driftwood beached and bleached. The lounge room floor is still buckled under its sandy regency carpet, but the room smells musty and old – no longer of perfume and Scotch and beer and tomato sandwiches. Or burnt steak – my grandmother was a terrible cook. Night after night, she would serve tough meat with tinned peas crushed with butter, lumpy mashed potato and stringy pumpkin. It was my mother who was the sophisticate. She'd pour Scotch from a crystal decanter she gave my grandparents one Christmas; and it was she who kept the tank-water ice topped up. She presented my grandmother with cosmetics each year – in frosted jars with lids studded with a glass topaz or emerald or amethyst – and my mother and grandmother were scented similarly of powder and had the same over-soft skin when I kissed them goodnight…

And the kitchen is the same, rows of primary-coloured cups hung on hooks above open shelves holding their matching saucers and sideplates. The rusted fridge with a hook to keep it closed is empty and smelly. I open the back door, but there is no familiar influx of stray cats.

I go into my grandmother's bedroom. Her bed is made up as I always remember it: in frothy lace turned down by satin-edged blankets. There are crystal trinket boxes in various shapes reflected in her rainbow-scalloped dresser mirror. And more paintings, everywhere.

I sit on the bed. What am I looking for? I hadn't meant to come here this weekend. Or had I? I did bring the key to the house with me. I feel restless and haunted.

I show Ross and Charlotte the grandchildren's bedroom, with its set of bunks and my old single bed, made up still with white cotton sheets and grey army surplus blankets; but they are more fascinated by a painted plywood mobile my brother Luke and I made once, in which fish still languidly swim. I show them then the store room with its treasure trove of *Boys' Own Annuals* from the 1940s, its untuned piano, its boxes of mothballed clothes and broken toys. They dig into boxes excitedly. I sit on the dusty floor and watch them.

And I think about Mark. I think about our honeymoon in this house. My grandparents were away, on holiday in Hong Kong, in their travelling phase. I remember one afternoon coming back from a run and finding Mark in the kitchen, in his board shorts, cutting up pieces of ginger and marinating prawns. His bare, bulky shoulders looked heavenly, all browned and toned from swimming and being in the sun, and when he turned to me, his beard was shining in curly black twists and his eyes were clear and happy, the blue flashing like water, or eager fish. He had swept the house and had hung out washing and had been learning new songs on his guitar.

'Your beauty is my salvation,' he said later, holding my chin with one hand and stroking my hair across my hip with the other, after we had made love and the dusk sun blew across his skin like a silk curtain.

And, with a spasm of pain – because it seems so long, so long since Mark has loved me like that – I remember thinking, no, no, you could be mine, you could be someone I else I can love, someone else who might truly love me: because Yanni had not come back and I had no faith any longer that he might.

Then I think about Yanni and me, here, long before Mark. I think about watching him at Main Beach, as I did so many times that summer: watching his long, brown body still as a cat's as a wave lifted its massive green bulk behind the thin wafer of his board; then his arms begin to move, to scoop green and white handfuls of sea in long, swift strokes; then the sudden spring, the impossibly swift leap onto his feet just as the wave peaked; and the airborne flight of his board, the wet gold flash of his golden head, and the curling, fearsome fingers of the tube softening to cradle him, to be nothing more dangerous than an unfurling banner, a long, flung, white and green unwinding streamer. Then that day, the day after the first time, watching him emerging from the sea, the muscles in his arm shining wet and silver around his board, his hair blindingly gold, his smile sheepish and seductive at once; and the morning breezy and hectic as we walked without touching to my grandmother's Mini, all the trees bowed under the lust of the wind – a good omen, I thought, and it was too: I let him drive and I put my hand on his knee, tracing my fingers up his thigh and he kept on driving and driving until he had to stop. We pulled off the road under the banksias and casuarinas and their sharp scent and the smell of the white sand blowing from the road verge against the car and in the broken window mixed with the salty smell of his body. His hands slid under my sarong and I had no knickers on and we pushed back the car seats and his eyelids were long and smooth like petalled bird wings, his voice husky…

And then we came demurely back here and he saluted my grandmother, who was working in her garden, and he'd shoved his surfboard under his arm and sauntered off down the beach to his parents' seafront home.

Then I watch the children playing with all the old things, sifting them through their fingers like time, and I know what I have come back here looking for. Love.

The water is cold but the children paddle and splash in it anyway. The tide is just on the turn. We walk along the narrow beach and across rocks to Yanni's house – but it is closed and silent and I don't even know whether his family still own it. We keep walking as far as we can go, then return. We make castles with the children's buckets and they decorate the turrets and walls with anything the tide has washed in: shells and pebbles, bits of weed and fragments of plastic, glass and cigarette packet. We all strip down to our swimmers and the sun is warm and the breeze light. The surf breaks on the faraway sandbank off to our right and the morning light spreads across the sea to the mountains of the mainland like a golden thrown cloth.

We return to Peri's house at eleven-thirty. We go around the outside of the house again, down the track that takes us to the back door. I don't want to get sand through the house – and that reluctance to enter the dark cavern of the upper storey still niggles at me.

Peri's in the lounge room, at an easel with her back to the light, working on a painting.

'Morning!' I say, pushing open the French door. 'Wipe your feet, children, and brush off the sand – okay, yes, now straight to the bathroom. Ross – you know how to run the bath – okay, off you go.'

Peri looks a little self-conscious – sheepish almost – as she turns to me. She grimaces and rolls her eyes, and picks up a rag to rub on the metal clasp of her paintbrush. 'Sorry I missed you this morning – I stayed up working on this thing after you went to bed. Sometimes it helps to have the alcohol-drenched perspective! But maybe not this time.'

I smile, shrugging. 'You don't think I know you?' I look curiously at the painting.

At first it seems to be only swirls of colour – black, spun with red and orange, a flicker of yellow, a flash of blue. Then I see that the picture is actually of a room, and that the colours are caused by light, perhaps sunset-light, because there are glimpses of prismatic colour filtering through reddish-black semi-transparent billowing curtains. And then in the centre of the billowing material I see a dark shadow, as if there is someone standing, behind the curtain, between the light and the room.

'Whoa,' I say. 'Is that the room upstairs? No, no –' because she is grimacing again – 'I like it. I really do. It's so strange…eerie.'

'Oh, I don't know. I can't seem to get the feeling right. That feeling of being threatened, and yet being drawn to the threat – sort of…powerful…' She's frowning, staring at the thing.

I am silent. There is something powerful in the painting – disturbing – but I'm not sure exactly what, or whether it's what she is trying to convey; but before I can answer, she gives her shoulders a shiver and dumps the paintbrush in a jar and turns to me, wiping her hands on the rag.

'So, where've you been?'

'Oh…on a trip down memory lane. Shouldn't have.' I turn away abruptly then: I don't really want to talk about the past, about any of the memories. They're too depressing.

'Oh?'

'I haven't been over here since Mark and I got married. Things change.'

'Mmm.' But she doesn't understand I'm not referring to things on the island.

'Can I cook something for lunch?' I say, to change the subject. 'How do bacon and egg burgers sound?' I make my voice cheerful.

Peri responds with a sudden, characteristic, flash of relief. 'Oh, God, fantastic. I'm starving.'

I cut up winter tomatoes, and lettuce and cucumber and avocado, and cook bacon and fry the eggs hard and flattened. I pile the colours on soft seedy rolls and Peri even has some plunger coffee; I take it out to the deck. We're all ravenous.

When we've finished eating, it's half-past twelve. The children bring out some colouring books and pens and we clear the plates to one side. The sea glistens like setting aspic and far out beyond the sandbank there is a blue boat with a cream sail. Peri and I sit in the warm sun and I feel suddenly drugged and slow. I feel suddenly as if I'd like to sleep…or at least lie quietly, my eyes half closed, watching the sea and drifting on memories.

I shake myself. I've got to snap out of it, I think. I've got to keep moving, doing things, otherwise I'll start dreaming, hoping, wishing…

I stand up abruptly and begin to stack the dishes. 'Now,' I say firmly, 'let's get these cleaned up and then go to Cylinder Beach this afternoon. For a swim. Ross's brought his boogie board and I've got Sharlie's arm-bands, but they'll need us as well in the surf.'

Peri looks a little sleepy and faraway too, but she raises her head to me as I speak and jerks it in agreement, then yawns. 'Okay,' she says through the yawn. 'It'll be my first swim since April, but if you're up to it, so am I.'

I smile at her and the children, whose heads are up, checking that I'm serious. 'Okay. And how about we go over to Main Beach and have a run on the sand dunes first, to warm up? Take some photos as well.'

And then I have to move, to carry the dishes inside and not look at Peri, because I'm sure my sudden interest in visiting surf beaches from my past must be as transparent as glass.

4

But I don't see anyone I know, or have known.

We do have a lovely time, nevertheless. The water is so cold it makes me gasp, but it exhilarates me. I squeal as loudly as Charlotte when a wave swamps us – it's as exciting as being on a roller coaster. Peri dolphin-dives into the waves and emerges with her perfect profile as sleek as silk, her hair slicked like a seal's to her head. I hold Charlotte in the rushing sea and my hair streams back, weightless – until I lift my head, and the hair is so heavy it might have beads braided into its ends.

We don't stay in too long, though. Charlotte chills quickly and I worry about Ross being dumped, because the waves are dumpers. That much I learned from Yanni, all those years ago. That, among other things.

Back at the house, Ross tries fishing with Peri's help, but he doesn't catch anything. 'It's the right place, but the wrong time of day,' he sighs as they bring the empty bucket back to Charlotte and me and our sand-castles.

I run another hot bath for the children and hop in too. They pour jugs of water over their heads and mine as we wash the sand out. It's luxurious and warm, with the small bathroom steamy and my wet hair around me like a cloak and Charlotte's little warm body curled under my chin. Luxurious especially because the scent of someone else's cooking seeps in under the door.

Over dinner, Peri says casually, 'How about we go up to the pub later?'

'I don't think so.' I say it too quickly; it's panic: fight or flight. My heart begins to thump. 'What would I do with the children? I hate seeing children in pubs. It's like putting roses in jam jars.'

'I could ring Judy, around at the Point.' She smiles, her voice and eyes suddenly bright. 'She loves children – hers are all grown – and she charges reasonable rates I've heard. Did make a few enquiries.' The smile broadens to a grin. 'I could ask her to pick up a video on the way? And they're probably exhausted.'

'A video, a video!' pipes Ross, animated. His voice always rises when he wants something he thinks he won't get.

'A video!' echoes Sharlie.

'Come on,' says Peri. 'Let's do it. You have to go back tomorrow. It's Saturday night. Everyone'll be there. Bet you don't get out much.'

'No.' My hands are actually shaking. 'Well, I guess we could go for a couple of hours.'

'Okay. I'll ring Judy, okay?'

'All right.'

Oh God, I think, what am I doing? How could I cope seeing him again? With Peri? Knowing Peri is in love with him, and that he might want her? And even if he doesn't, what could it possibly achieve anyway, even if I did speak to him and we talked about why he left and…

But both my logic and imagination are swamped in a flood of adrenalin I am powerless to resist.

We change and put on make-up. I feel sick with fear, or hope.

Charlotte is already asleep on the couch by the time we're ready to leave.

'I'll look after her, Mum,' says Ross absently, watching the film Judy's brought.

'Don't you worry about them,' Judy says to me. 'If they're good, I might take them down to the beach in the morning and see if we can catch a fish with that line of theirs.'

'Huh?' Ross swings to face her.

'You bet. I haven't lived on this island for twenty years without catching a fish or two. Got some bait?' Judy has crinkled brown skin around her eyes and wears a denim jacket embroidered with flowers and mirrors. Her face is kind and her body comfortable. She has dark brown hair streaked with silver. Her husband is off fishing with his mates himself; she's brought with her the beads and shells which she threads into jewellery for a local shop.

'Got some worms left!'

'They'll do. Catch whiting with that.'

Ross begins to wriggle with excitement, his whole body turned from the screen to her.

'You watch the rest of the movie now. Then I'll pop you into bed so's we can be up early.' She turns to Peri and me. 'Don't you hurry back. I'll stay the night. Kip down on this – sofa bed, isn't it?'

Peri's pushing earrings through her lobes. 'Are you sure? I mean, we'll be able to drop you back – one of us has to drive anyway…or if you do want to stay, there's plenty of beds upstairs – '

'Ta, but there's no one to go home to tonight. Boys won't be back till morning. Just as soon stay here. And I don't fancy them beds upstairs. Too dark and gloomy up there. Remember this place from when the last people owned it – sort of a guesthouse it was. Used to give me the creeps, even then.' She licks the end of a piece of fishing line and carefully strings a bead.

'Oh well, if you want – there are sheets and blankets in here –'

'Ta. I'll find 'em. Now off you go and stop fussing.'

I pick up Sharlie to take her to bed, and bend and kiss Ross. 'You be good, now, won't you? As if you won't be, with fishing to look forward to! Thanks, Judy. You know where we are if…'

'Yeah, yeah, I know. They'll be fine. Just go!'

There is only one pub at Point Lookout. When I was a teenager, RSL clubs and sporting clubs served beer and wine with bingo and bowls in halls in the townships, and I bought Summer Wine and Green Ginger Wine over the counter from such places, which Yanni and I drank from the bottle on the beach. The clubs are still there, and more, but the pub is the main focal point for the island's social life.

There is a sealed road all the way from the ferry terminal at Dunwich to the pub, and from there to Main Beach, the treacherous, rite of passage for all would-be surfers. There the sealed road ends. The house Peri is staying in is off the sealed road, between Amity on the western side where my grandmother's house is and the pub which faces full north. The road from her place roughly follows the coast, through undeveloped forest for the most part, but it only takes us ten minutes, and one kangaroo shying away from our lights, to get to the sealed section. Another five minutes brings us to the Point Lookout Hotel.

I take a deep breath as we climb the steps to the beer garden. Another. I concentrate on the smells – of hops and cigarettes, of bodies and bated excitement – of an exuded lust for the unexpected...

But one quick glance tells me Yanni is not there.

We find a table in the beer garden. Peri goes up to the garden bar to order drinks and I look around, more calmly, not sure whether I'm relieved or disappointed.

It is much more elaborate than I remember: it has been revamped – replacing its original simplicity with an upmarket smartness. The old slatted timber tables and bench seats have been sanded and painted slate-grey; there are newcomers too: round, rickety plastic tables and stackable plastic chairs. Potted palms stand as discreetly as good waiters among them. There is a sandpit in the twisted stand of brushbox which shades the beer garden in the daytime; three little hooded children are chasing each other among the tree's branches, ignoring the buckets and spades in the pit. Lights in the tree shift across the children through the filigree of upper twigs, and I smile because the children could be elves with their hoods and scampering limbs. I look beyond them and there is the view exactly as I remember it: a great dark swath of sea, waves unfurling from far out like a silver-blond fall of hair released from curling pins, and spray fanning up in the moonlight from a sinister black hump of rock almost buried by the tide.

Midnight Oil are singing from loudspeakers. A tall, red-eyed man with a brown beard comes among the tables with a hose, spraying the pot plants. Water splashes on my feet.

Peri comes back with two glasses of beer. We sip quietly. There is a table of six near us, two girls and four boys. The boys are all dressed in surfing sweaters and jeans and the girls in jeans and loose jumpers. They are talking about a fancy dress party they are to go to. Obviously they're not in costume yet. 'Gross,' I hear. 'Spinnin'.' 'Coo-al.'

Suddenly one of the boys leans over to me and places a hot, hard hand on my forearm. 'Filthy eyes,' he says, staring. His breath is close and beery.

'Same to you,' I say, even though his eyes are washed as cleanly blue as the sea.

'Hey,' he says, still staring at me, 'don't I know you?'

'Can't you think of anything more original?'

'Huh?' His eyes might be bright and beautiful, but what's behind them isn't too high voltage. He moves his palm down my arm, to my hand. 'Married, hey?'

'Too old for you, in any case.'

'I dunno. Like 'em older – like 'em married. Like 'em warm and wet and hungry.' He smiles slowly and his hot paw closes around my hand.

I stare at him and to my horror feel my body brim up with desire. There's something pure and animal and magnetic about him – something primitive, something I thought I was immune to, something I thought I had trained myself out of long ago.

'Get lost, creep,' I say quickly, as coldly as I can. I shake off his arm and roughly pull my chair away from him. 'Let's move tables.' I hear a girl at his table laugh. I feel shaky; my heart is pounding.

'You all right?' Peri says when we have moved to safer ground. 'Nothing's sacred around here. It's a pagan island. Different rules.' She smiles suddenly. 'It's contagious. Maybe that's what's affecting me.'

I look at her sharply then, but she swings her gaze away quickly.

I want to say, what do you mean? But I sense she'll clam up on me. We're cousins: we know each other well; but that doesn't mean she'll trust me with the finer details of her life.

She's looking around the beer garden. All the tables I can see have people sitting at them now, but her face doesn't register recognition of any of them. They seem like a youngish crowd mainly – brown-skinned, looking as if there is still a trace of salt on their skin; casually dressed, drinking jugs of beer, smoking – as you would expect; then there are some older couples and a group of women with children. I wonder absently where their men are. In the public bar, watching football on Sky TV, probably. I look back at Peri. She's running her hand up and down her beaded glass of beer.

'So,' I say, taking a breath, feeling at last as if I can ask this question casually, 'tell me more about Yanni. Where you met him again over here. How he is. You know.'

She relaxes a little and her attention shifts back to me. And of course he's her favourite subject – of course talking about him animates her, makes her glow. I passively watch that happen to her, and there's an ache in my chest that's jealousy, but empathy, too.

'I ran into him when I was camping with other students at Easter. Oh God, he's so…' She trails off, and I know why. He's not an easy person to describe. 'I recognised him straightaway when I walked into his shop. My boogie board had snapped and I wanted another one. At first he didn't remember who I was, but when I mentioned you, it clicked.'

My heart beats a little faster and I nod and sip my beer. A new song starts over the loudspeakers, but it's just background noise, like the static of voices around us and sudden surges of cheering from the television in the public bar.

'Then I ran into him on the beach. And here, at the pub. All the locals know each other, of course. Which is probably why none of them are here tonight. They're probably all at some party. They can be cliquey.'

So she's not really in with the locals, then, I think. Perhaps there's a period of trial before that happens. Oh maybe you need to be someone's girlfriend to get in. I'm familiar with that way of thinking, from living in country towns. So maybe if she was Yanni's girlfriend, he could fulfil many of her needs: give her access to the in-crowd, give her security here, relieve loneliness, give her the back-up to continue defying her mother. I don't even want to think about the obvious one – make her delirious, drunk with happiness... I feel my heart slowing, sinking. I should be hoping for these things for her, not hoping Yanni would see me and...what? I'm not even game to imagine.

'But he made a point of talking to me. Introducing me to people. That's how I found out about spare rooms, places to stay cheaply. Probably would have been happy to stay with the last woman I lived with – Ruth – except that she left. Went back to the mainland and the lease on the place ran out. And then Haden came up with the offer of his place.'

And I switch back. I have a new surge of hope. It sounds innocent, the way she describes it. It sounds as if Yanni was just being polite, chivalrous, without real sexual interest.

And I'm just about to bite the bullet, ask if he's made any moves, when the surfie who talked to me earlier suddenly looms beside us. He has a jug of beer in his hand.

'You girls want some of this?'

'No,' I say, quickly, not looking at him.

Peri hesitates, then shakes her head too. He goes away.

But the moment has been temporarily lost.

I pause, recognise this, then say, 'It's my shout, though. Same again?'

Peri nods and drains her glass.

When I come back, Peri smiles at me almost impishly.

'What's up?' I say.

'I was just thinking. Maybe you should have let him buy you a drink.'

'Who, that guy? After what he said to me?' My heart quickens again at the memory.

'Well...things between you and Mark don't seem to be getting any better. From what you said last night.'

I had opened up a bit, I recall with a touch of guilt.

'Maybe you should just...I don't know, have a bit of a fling. What harm could it do? Mark would never find out.'

I stare at her. Unbidden, something that happened to me a week ago comes back. One of Mark's friends, Grant, dropped in to borrow some of Mark's tools. Mark was out and I made Grant a cup of tea while he was waiting. Our hands touched as I passed him the cup and saucer. He held my gaze. He had soft brown eyes... I panicked, moved away; that was the end of it. But that night I dreamed of Grant: I dreamed I was massaging his wife's neck and then he did as well; then Grant's hand touched mine and he turned to me and began to kiss me – kisses I drowned in; his hands were strong, slim, hot on my body – and his wife was oblivious. And I woke up with my heart pounding and desire like a drug in my veins.

I pondered my reaction all day. I didn't find Grant particularly attractive. He was strong-looking, with broad, competent hands, but his face was narrow with thick black eyebrows. What was wrong with me, that I'd have a sexual dream about a man I didn't even find desirable? Just because he looked at me in a certain way? Maybe it was hormones. Maybe it was sexual frustration with Mark, who was retiring more and more to his shed in the evenings. Maybe it was boredom. Maybe it was an early seven-year-itch.

I grimace. 'You've been living with these pagans too long. Whether Mark found out or not is hardly the issue! That's not all there is to it. I'd know, and then I'd feel guilty – and besides, I don't even like that guy!'

She puts her head on one side. 'But what if you did?'

I hesitate. She's looking at me with her eyebrows raised, sipping her drink. Is she asking me about Yanni? I wonder. Has she realised there's still something there – has Yanni said anything to her? How close are they?

I shrug, defensive. 'Well, you'd have to think about Aids, syphilis.'

'Condoms.'

'Gossip. *The Scarlet Letter*.'

'Attention to detail.'

'Fear.'

'Ah!'

'I'm not all that young any more. Insecurity.'

'Believe me, that's the least of your worries.'

'Starting something I won't be able, or want, to finish. Jeopardising everything I have.'

'Gold over love.'

'Love? Who said anything about love? We're on about lust here, aren't we?'

'Yeah, well, you have to have lust to have love, don't you? And if there's no lust or love left with Mark…'

'I didn't say that!'

'No.' She looks at me expectantly.

I sigh. 'Okay. There's not much there at the moment, I admit. Not now. But it's the kids – they demand so much of my time and he's really busy at work –'

'Stop making excuses for him.'

We stare at each other.

'The thing is,' I say slowly, 'that I don't think I could do it without falling in love. It's love I look for, not sex. Sex doesn't mean anything to me unless I can get under the skin, under the flesh, into the essence…'

And she's nodding. Her expression is resigned. It's how she sees it too, I can tell.

And then she looks up at someone behind me, her eyes widening, then creasing into a smile.

5

But it's only the surfie again. He has a full jug of beer and his smile is lazy. 'Come on,' he says, placing the jug on the table. 'Have a beer. Can't drink all this on me own.'

I glance at his table: his friends are gone.

'Okay, thanks,' says Peri, before I have a chance to say anything. 'Have a seat.'

I raise my eyebrows at her, but she won't look at me. I grudgingly move my chair around. My heartbeat is normalising.

The surfie is looking at me. His hair is sun-bleached and sticky-looking, but he does have lovely eyes. 'From Brisbane?'

'Mmm,' I murmur, 'for the weekend.'

'Can always tell by the shoes.'

I look down at my red stilettos. 'It's fashionable to wear these with jeans.' I'm a bit defensive. I glance at Peri again, but she's gazing innocently out to sea.

'Into fashion, are ya?'

I shrug, and grimace: then look at him steadily. 'I'm a conformist, I guess. Looks like you are too.'

But the jibe goes right over his head. 'Know why I thought I'd seen you before.' He's nodding, pushing back the sticky hair.

'Yeah?' I'm offhand.

'Yeah...you look like – what's that actress's name...'

I sigh. Alcohol does this to men, I've noticed before: talk about rose-coloured glasses...

'Michelle Pfeiffer!'

I roll my eyes. 'Now that's a new one... But no. No. I don't look like Michelle Pfeiffer. I wish I did, but I don't...'

He catches my hair, which I've tied back in a ponytail. 'Is it real?'

'Hey!' He's yanked it. 'Course it's real! Do you mind?' I glare at him, then twist with my head on one side to Peri, who's watching us now, just the shadow of a smile on her face.

She says, 'I remember you. Mick, isn't it?'

Mick refills our glasses. 'Hey, you girls want to come to a party? Fancy dress, over at Jacko's. His girlfriend's birthday.'

'Oh yeah, what are you going as? A surfer?' It's a weak jab I know, but I'm not feeling together enough to be witty.

'Nah. Just goin' to grab a branch off a tree, stick it down the back of me shirt and go as a shady character.'

And we can't help laughing, and suddenly the mood is lightened. Mick looks pleased with himself.

'How about it?' Peri's eyes are alight. 'If he can come up with that, we can come up with anything.'

I don't feel like going home; I admit that to myself. I look at Peri, not the surfie. 'I guess we could go for a little while. You know this Jacko?'

'Met him. You get to know most people up here after a while.' She's leaning forward, her eyes bright and deep.

The anticipation I've been quelling rises in my throat.

'Good on ya!'

Peri drains her glass. 'Let's get some takeaways,' she says briskly. 'What time's the party start?'

'Been going since seven.'

Peri gives me an I-told-you-so look. 'See you there, then.'

'You bet.'

I smile at him because he looks a little bemused, and his conquest will after all be short-lived. But he's cute enough for it not to worry me too much.

We decide to head down to the beach below the pub to forage around for something inspiring to wear. Mick's set a precedent: we have to at least make an effort now too.

Peri leads the way down a track which winds through boulders and spiky pandanus trees. The moon is nearly full and shines like silver paint on black wet rocks below. I can see my path well – but even so I snag a heel almost immediately on a tree root. This gives me an idea. I pull off my shoes and backtrack to a clump of gum trees we passed on the headland; I snap off twigfuls of leaves. Then I clamber down to the beach. I can see Peri trekking towards the brush on the edge of the sand. I sit on dry rocks where Peri can see me and I plait the leaves in a wreath.

'Any luck?' I call presently when Peri is within earshot.

She's got armfuls of something. 'Yeah! How about you?'

I wait till she can flop down beside me. 'Look at this,' I say. I place the plaited wreath around my head, under my ponytail. 'I'm Achilles. These are my heels.' I hold up the red stilettos.

Peri hoots. 'Well, I'm spring! Can you believe there are so many flowers out already?' She pulls the band from her fountain of black hair and combs it with her fingers, then she begins to push bottlebrush blooms, tiny closed daisies and sprigs of early wattle into it and into the weave of her loose-knit sweater. 'Open one of those bottles, will you?' she says, still busy.

We've bought two bottles of sparkling wine; she's left them in their white plastic bag in a rock pool nearby. I pop a cork into the sea, take a swig and hand her the bottle. She looks weird – elfin – with all the flowers and her dark hair wispy around her face. She looks elfin and wild and free. I look down at my Achilles heels and suppress a sudden sigh.

'We might as well walk to the party,' she says. It's just down at Cylinder Beach. Across the road. Been there before – they're always having parties.' She takes another swig, then pulls herself upright. 'Come on, let's get there.'

I sit still for just a second, then I gather my heels and the rest of the wine and follow her through the squeaky, moon-washed sand to Cylinder Beach.

A spotlight slung from the trunk of a tree throws up weird images from the party, like snatches of a surreal song. They've made an effort, these island people: a tube of toothpaste is gyrating with an evil-looking figure in black labelled 'plaque'; there's a newspaper, complete with white centre band to keep it rolled up, headed for the ice and drink-filled laundry tubs under the house; and there's someone I can identify with, I think – an Icarus, his face painted silver and his wings dragging forlornly, as if his journey to the sun is already over.

Oasis is playing. We don't see Mick, but Peri strides confidently in. I follow her through the bodies flickering shadows in long swaths from the spotlight. Peri finds us clear plastic glasses near the laundry tubs and we pour drinks. The sparkling wine tastes tart and cheap, but it's cold enough.

A woman comes up to us. She has short, dark hair and false eye-lashes, and someone has painted a vista over one side of her face. 'I'm Michelle,' she says. 'It's my party.'

I'm not sure whether that's an accusation or a welcome, but Peri handles things anyway. 'I remember you,' she says. 'Been here before. Jacko's twenty-fifth. Peri. This is Ven.' She turns to me.

'Hi.'

'Want some of this?' Peri asks. She pours wine into Michelle's half-full glass. 'Ran into Mick at the pub. Liked the look of Ven, I think. Great costumes.'

'What are yous?'

'I'm spring, Ven's Achilles. The heels, you know.' Michelle looks down at my feet suspiciously. 'What are you?'

'Dunno. Just something different. You know how long it took to paint my face? Two hours. It was murder. Couldn't smile or talk or nuthin'. All right. Have a good time, won't yous?'

'Yeah – happy birthday.'

'Ta.' She drifts away into the unreal light.

I can see Icarus again, threading his way through the dancers towards us – or more probably the laundry tubs. He's tall and the silver on his face makes him stand out as well. As he gets closer, I see his wings are made of negligees, with black feathers sketched on them. They have rents in them and smears of some dark stain – Icarus after the fall, surely, then. He has on a black mesh shirt and I can't help staring at the swell of silver-gold muscle gleaming through it as the fluorescent laundry light touches him... He must have been dancing, I think, to have such a sheen – and his silver face is sculptured too, as perfectly planed as a cartoon hero's...

And then I recognise that face. Yanni.

Peri has realised too: she's turned to him, her face lifted and shining; and when she says his name, her voice is soft and sweet, all the previous briskness drained from it.

But he's looking at me, and my heart is so violent I think my hand will shake if I lift my glass. He is smiling at me, his eyes sharp and green, a thatch of hair as blond as wheat falling to one side of his face. I stare at him, at the cleft in his chin, the slanted eyelids – and at the pianist hand lifted to brush the hair from his eye, the hand whose fingers I have licked and kissed, fingers which have entered me, whose palm has sucked my nipples, kneaded my thighs – and my knees are weak with fear.

So when he speaks, the formal tone of his voice shocks me. 'Venny. I thought it was you. How are you?' He's smiling, but uncertainly. His hand doesn't reach out, doesn't touch me...

As if it hasn't been eleven years since we've seen each other. As if there's nothing, never has been, anything between us. As if there were no promises made, no history of childhood love, adolescent love, physical love, spiritual love...

But before I can answer, Peri catches his hand and he turns automatically to her, and his smile becomes more certain – and I tip my glass, frightened.

'Thought you might be here.' Peri's looking at him, her eyes bright and deep again.

'Well, I got roped into it.'

'Sure. Like you don't like to party.'

'Any more than you do.'

'On a Saturday night.'

Her eyes seem to blaze, despite their darkness, despite the ordinariness of the laundry light, and he's smiling teasingly back. Their intimacy brings the wine up in my throat. I almost gag, turning away to duck my mouth – to face Mick.

He's grinning happily, the shady branch as promised flopping over his head. He has lazy, happy eyes and a drunken smile.

'Made it then, huh? Didn't reckon you would. Thought you'd be too stuck-up. What're ya drinkin'?'

I straighten, swallowing, and take a breath. I'm so relieved by the distraction I could laugh, except I'm so frightened. 'Oh, wine,' I answer, looking vaguely for the bottle, not game to turn back to the others.

He finds it and refills my glass, then Peri's. I'm forced to turn into their circle.

'So what're yous supposed to be?' He's addressing me again.

'Achilles.' I semi-smile at him. 'Remember my heels? My Achilles heels.'

He looks at me vacantly. I glance quickly at Yanni.

And Yanni's half-smile is a little perplexed. 'Achilles?' he says, his head on one side.

'Pretty obscure, I know, but the best I could do with half an hour's notice. But you're Icarus, surely?'

'Icarus? No, I'm just a bird.' He's shaking his head. He's turned to face me fully, but Peri still holds his arm.

'Oh, it's just...' I stare at him, and I feel so stupid, so ridiculously naive – of course he wouldn't have dressed as a Greek mythical creature – that game, that silly private game that we used to play, that private world we inhabited, that no longer exists, it's past, part of childhood, lost –

And then his face relaxes and the old, old dreaminess is there. 'Well,' he says, 'I could be Icarus. After all, what bird has a silver face? Has such foolish wings?'

'And all those rents and tears…'

'And dirt. What self-respecting bird would let his wings drag in the dirt?'

'You've had a bit of a fall. Still testing the wings…'

'Trying new horizons. New skies.' His smile is dreamy and teasing, the way I remember it. Then he sings, very low, very softly, 'I am Pegasus…'

'My name means horse,' I sing back just as softly. And it's as if the others have vanished.

And the others haven't heard the words anyway. Only Yanni is looking at my mouth, because Mick is speaking, leaning toward Peri.

'I know what you are! Spring. Arn'cha?'

And Peri smiles radiantly, her pink fingernails digging lightly into the mesh sleeve on Yanni's arm. She's beautiful and sprite and her hair is wispy as a wood nymph's and as enchanting, with its threads of flowers.

But I have known Yanni for a long, long time.

'Mmm,' Peri's saying; 'couldn't believe there'd be so many flowers around. It's still winter really. Supposed to be. Maybe the flowers are fooled by the rain. And it's quite warm – isn't it warm for winter?'

The music surges suddenly, cranked up for the popular hit – 'I don't believe that anybody feels the way I do…about you now…' The whole party, it seems, is suddenly singing along.

Mick grabs me by the arm. 'C'min dance!' he yells, over the voices. His eyes are sparkling blue in the red pool of beer he's drunk.

'Okay!' I yell back.

I don't take off my Achilles heels. I dance in my red, high shoes and my heart is singing. I pull the scrunchie from my high ponytail and my hair hangs loose and long and light in its wreath of leaves, and I feel as if I am eighteen again and all the possibilities of life are opening like ripples from the thrown pebble of Yanni's smile…

But when I look back to where Yanni was standing, I see that he is gone; and a heavy man in a long, dark coat is standing over Peri, his back to me, his shadow cast over her face.

6

I falter in the dance. I watch them. Peri has her head thrown back, but her expression is invisible in his shadow. All that strikes me is that with all the flowers caught in her hair she looks suddenly like a trapped wood nymph. Goosebumps brush across my shoulders.

Then the man shifts and the shadow moves from her face, and I see Peri is frowning and speaking. And then she drops her head and turns with him – to go out of the laundry, away from where I can see her, away from the party, into darkness.

Unreasonably, I am struck with panic. Maybe it's just the size of the man – formidable beside slight, fragile Peri – or the vaguely threatening air the long black coat gives him. Maybe it's the fact that she was frowning, and has gone with him, without a glance in my direction. I push through the throng of bodies – nearly everyone's dancing now the music's so loud – turning briefly to wave to Mick. He looks after me in mild surprise, but nothing much else registers on his face.

I push out to the laundry light, then stumble past it and into the darkness which has swallowed them. 'Peri?' I shout: but my voice sounds weak and useless, lost like a birdcall in the whip of music.

No one answers. My eyes adjust slowly to the moonlight I've fallen into. There's no one I can see there, no shapes, nothing. Only a dark spread of lawn and the black strip of road with cars parked along it.

'Ven.'

I flick my head sharply. He's standing quite close but behind me, under the still winter branches of a poinciana tree, and the moon crazes his silver face with bare branch shadows. He comes over to me, his torn wings trailing. I wonder suddenly whose negligees he used to make them…

'Did you see Peri and some man come out?' I ask it sharply, because he's out here, perhaps following her too, and because the panic is still in my throat: but again the words and tone are lost to the music.

He lowers his head to mine, and I smell rum on his breath, and I repeat the question, shouting in his ear. He nods. 'His name's Haden,' he yells back at me.

'You know him?'

'Oh, everyone does. Throws his money around a bit – but where he gets it from is pretty sus. She's living in his house.'

The Oasis song suddenly finishes, and the silence is crisp and ringing.

'What do you mean, 'sus'?' I ask, my voice suddenly quiet and clear.

He looks down at me, and I can see the hesitation in his face. Then he shrugs. 'Drugs, maybe.'

'What...marijuana?' I'm relieved. That's just supply and demand on this island, surely...

'Uh, uh. I'm talking white stuff.' He's lifted his head to frown at the road again.

'But Peri's not into that... I know her! What does he want with her?'

'Don't know.' His voice is barely more than a mutter now. 'They're going in a car. Look.'

And too late I see headlights pull onto the road, a flash of gold paint, and then the twin red taillights.

'Don't like him much.'

And it's selfish and stupid, but at that I'm stabbed with jealousy. Because Yanni seems worried about Peri, seems to care for her. And I should be happy about that, that there's someone looking out for her: and if it were anyone other than Yanni, I would be.

'She's a big girl,' I mutter.

'What?'

The music – a Cold Chisel number this time – has just started up again, but more moderately. Even so, it blocks out my voice.

'Oh, nothing.' I'm relieved he hasn't heard me; because of course I don't mean it – I am concerned about her: it's just his concern I can't stand. I jerk my head up. 'Where do you think they might have gone?'

'I don't know.' He's looking out, down the road, still frowning.

'Well, they could've gone for a smoke or something,' I say cautiously.

But why would she have been frowning about that?

'Mmm,' he says. 'So she is into mull, then?'

And I think, at least you don't know that much about her. 'Well,' I say, 'she has been known to have the odd toke.' Likes it particularly with sex, I'm on the verge of saying – but realise in time that that would be catty. And not even perhaps true – it's me who likes it with sex. But he probably doesn't remember that.

And suddenly I'm thinking about him, remembering him, in our cave, me kneeling over him, his body spread under mine on my sarong, languid, his eyelids heavy, his palms open above his white-blond head, as I hold the last of the joint to his lips, then take it in mine, then crush it out in the sand; and I gently run my fingernails along the golden swell of his hairless chest, around his ribs and into his belly and slowly down to his groin, and then lower myself, slippery, around him…

I shift my eyes back to his silver face and wait quietly, until he looks at me. And I watch his eyes come to rest on my face, and the frown dissipate like steam. And he's looking fully at me, his eyes dark in the shadows of the poinciana, and I can't read their expression, but his body seems to melt somehow then, to curve down and around me, over me; and I have such an impulse to curl into his wings that I have to step backwards.

'Let's get out of here.' He jerks his head up, suddenly decisive. 'Come on. It's too noisy. Let's go to – well, let's see if you remember.' His voice is trailing with his wings, because he's walking away, towards the road.

I hesitate for just a second, then I pull off my Achilles heels and follow him.

I catch up and we walk along the sandy shoulder of the road, away from Cylinder Beach, away from my car parked up at the pub, away from where Peri will expect to find me when she comes back. Because of course she will come back. But I don't want to think about her, I refuse to feel guilty about her; I think, this is something I have to do: I have to find out why he never came back – that's all I'm doing – I'm just going to talk to him, get him to talk to me. I glance up at his face and I know instinctively that he'll ignore me if I say anything yet, that I have to be patient and let him lead – or maybe that's not instinct: maybe I remember that reaction from another time…

I have to stride fast to keep up with him, so I don't have much breath for talking, anyway. The moonlight creams the sand and glints on the black sealed road as we cross it.

He finds a track without difficulty. It winds crookedly through soft-brushed casuarinas. He walks ahead of me, in silence, in the dappled dark; and gradually my teaming brain slows and calms.

I'm suddenly conscious of the cold night wind blowing in from the sea. We're getting close to the beach. Yanni must be freezing, I think suddenly, practically, in only that black mesh… Then he breaks through to the beach and full moonlight, and I stumble after him over a sand dune –

And I know where we are.

I stand still and look at him, his tall, lean back and moon-washed hair, his wings fluttering gently in the night wind; and I look out at the softly breaking sea, the waves smooth and small in the protected cove. I look at him and know why he has brought me here, to this particular cove again, and it is as if the past eleven years – Mark, my children, everything – have vanished.

I think only of the day I met him, the first day I came here, swam here, drifted into this cove and into his life.

The call was like that of a seabird, high on the wind. 'Okay, yeah, you ready now? Now wait for it – now!' Yanni was on his board, his arms flexed and frozen, the eleven-year-old muscles of his calves like carved wax. Luke, my brother, was on his board too, but his arms were flailing, his feet searching the board for balance. Yanni was way ahead of him, swooping along the underbelly of the wave until it began to smooth out; then he flicked the board swiftly into a turn and dived into its glossy back. Luke was surfacing close to where he'd started, his board bouncing in the foam.

I ducked under the next wave and swam away from them, away from the point, into a cove where the breakers flattened into long, low, spread sheets of green water, and you could lie with only the gas-blue sky in your eyes and the rush of the sea in your ears and the hot, bright light on your face.

Luke could look after himself. He had the knack.

I had problems of my own. Sister problems, puberty problems, parent problems. Adjustment problems. We'd just moved town again – for the tenth time in my thirteen years – and I was sick to the heart at even the thought of a new school in two weeks. A new school, a new class – a grade nine class. Not a grade eight class, where many kids didn't know each other anyway, nor a year ten class, where everyone would be preparing for change at the end of the year, but smack bang between them, in no-new-kid's land. And to make matters worse I'd grown into some sort of overgrown puppy: my feet were too big, my hands too long, my body too thin.

I'd already decided that year I would be mute. In some of the harder years of primary school I'd already experimented with the invisibility muteness brings. It had worked to a surprising extent: but who after all takes any notice of, or later remembers, someone who never speaks and who is at their school for less than a year? And who never later appears in class photos, because, somehow, she is always between schools when they're taken? Even at the time I felt myself quite invisible: I could passively study faces, back of necks, of heads, watch children answering questions, skipping, eating, playing with balls, writing, slipping strands of hair behind an ear, passing notes – and know that I did not really exist there at all.

So that year, my fourteenth year, I'd again be mute. I'd go to school and work in class and spend my lunchtimes in the library and my afternoons at ballet lessons – the one 'sport' I'd discovered which involved absolutely no vocal input on my part – or practising the painting techniques my father was teaching me. Then I'd eat dinner and do homework and go to bed. And on the weekends I'd read and practise new steps and watch my father's silent brushwork.

I wouldn't have to talk to anyone, not really. Especially not my elder sister, who picked up friends like bindi-eyes in a spring backyard and who despised me for my social ineptitude – and for a myriad other sibling rivalry reasons we have long since given up trying to resolve.

But none of that really helped the sick-at-heart feeling.

'Hey!'

The voice startled me, approaching so suddenly; I fell from my floating trance and stumbled for a foothold, but the water was too deep. I surfaced to Yanni, lying facedown on his board and smiling happily at me.

'Want to have a go?'

'What, at surfing?' I grabbed hold of the edge of his board.

'Yeah.'

'You've got to be kidding!'

'Come on, it's not so hard.'

'Easy for you to say. Want me to teach you to pirouette?'

He laughed and his eyes were so beautiful I couldn't help smiling back. They were water-bright, liquid aquamarine, the colour of a stream running over white pebbles in the sun, and they had dark circles around the green and his lashes were heavy and dark and wet from the sea. I thought then, for the first time, that those eyes could one day break my heart.

I sit down on the sand dune. It's loose and cold, but soft. Yanni has turned and is looking at me instead of the sea with its moon-trail of silver. It's very quiet, only the hushed waves breathing rhythmically. He comes back to me and stretches his legs out beside mine; then we both look silently out to sea.

That summer I met him was also the summer that marked the beginning of my parents' 'settling down' period. My father was an artist and up until then had moved restlessly from town to town, painting the local landscapes and the towns, establishing a reputation for his style and his personality. But now they'd come back to Brisbane, to settle, and settle us, Shelley, Luke and me, into schools and into a regular life.

Only for me it was too late. The years of dislocation had had their toll. I felt I couldn't fit in anywhere; I was forever an outsider.

Except on North Stradbroke Island. Holidays at Amity, at my grandparents' house, had been the only constant event in my childhood, and I loved and clung to the place as if it were my territory, my land. So once we moved to Brisbane, an hour's car-ferry ride from Stradbroke, I began to spend weekends there, usually with Luke tagging along because he was wild about surfing, often the whole family as well; and holidays, summer, winter, autumn and spring.

So I began to know Yanni, because Yanni was on the island most weekends, staying with his parents at their beach house just one hundred metres away from my grandparents, and Yanni and Luke had become friends.

I used to go with them when they surfed. Yanni was an only child and his mother was devoted to him. She would drive them at dawn to a surf beach and I'd go too because I liked the solitude of those early hours – I could explore the headland, the beaches, the National Parks without fear of company, listen to bird calls and stretch the ache for what I couldn't identify from my young body; then I could lie on the beach and feel the soft morning sun like scent on my skin, and watch the changing colours of the sky and the sea and the clouds. I could brown my body slowly and read, or watch my brother and his beautiful friend learn to harness the waves – learn the harnessing of them as boys in the country towns I'd lived in learned to harness horses, or the land.

After they were exhausted, they'd come back and throw themselves on towels beside me. And then we'd talk. About Luke and my past:

about the towns we'd lived in, the horrors of having a famous father, the blur of schools we'd been to. And about Yanni's past.

Yanni was born in Greece. Both his parents were Australian, but his mother had had a contagious fascination for Greece, and his father a reckless, adventurous spirit (which I recognised, too, in Yanni): so his parents bought a little taverna in Kalymnos. At the time, such things were cheap and the lifestyle wonderful.

Yanni was taken to England when he was two because money was low and his father was offered a well-paid job; but they returned to Greece when Yanni was seven. And it was then I think his particular character, and particular charisma, took shape. With his white-blond hair, he was unique on the island: and from the time he and his parents arrived, a stream of shrieking children would pour behind them whenever they moved from the dark recesses of their taverna... and so began his certain knowledge in his absolute exceptionality, in all his blond power over a dark and superstitious people... He was a king, a favourite of the gods...

Then as his freedom developed, so did his free child's capacity to extend his body, to stretch the limits of his imagination, and prove without doubt that his supremacy was justified. By the time he was ten and Greek politics had become a problem for foreigners, and he and his parents had to return to Australia, his nature had been formed.

But he did love Kalymnos with a passion. He spoke of its caves and inlets, its swimming holes and thermal springs, its ruined villages and temples and churches. He knew all its rituals and rites, its old stories and legends. He spoke of climbing barefoot and barely clad among ruined marble pillars and milk thistles, wild herbs and flowers and wheat, over slabs of mountain with skins like grey elephants, through groves of figs hung with rich syrupy fruit, under almond and olive orchards smelling woody and dry and hot. He spoke of wandering dusty tracks with belled black goats and spotted pigs and thin, tattered cats. He spoke of the hot, enamelled blue of the sky and the sapphire of the Aegean: dropping into that sea like a seabird from a rock edge into indigo coolness; then coming up, currents weaving like cats around his ankles; and then floating on his back while the sea roared in his ears and swallows and gulls and albatross wheeled against the sky ... Did he really say these things, or was it only as I saw them in my imagination? Whatever the truth, the sound of the waves and the heat and quiet, dreaming peace of those times we lay on the beach, unskeining our memories and perhaps embroidering and exaggerating them, combined to create a magic in both our pasts.

And led me to learn to surf. I was fifteen, feeling savagely miserable, lying in my private cove, thinking about Shelley up at the clubhouse at Main Beach the day before, flaunting her ripe body – and about Luke, who was floundering in the surf, letting the side down while Yanni skimmed the waves, light as an ice skater – and about me, fifteen and still growing. Growing tall. Too tall. Not petite and light and tiny, as a dancer should be, had to be, but tall. Too, too tall. Thinking about the crumbling of my future and the hopelessness of dreams.

Then Yanni came out of the water and flopped down on his towel beside me and I saw with surprise that he was as tall as I was. 'Surf's perfect,' he said. 'Perfect just there for beginners. Reckon you should have a go.'

He'd nagged me a few times before. Maybe because he loved it so much he thought everybody would once they tried it. I'd watched them often enough to have an inkling of what to do, but also to know that what was required to succeed was a courage I didn't possess. But I felt suddenly reckless with my misery. 'All right,' I said.

I had good balance from ballet, and that perhaps, combined with the recklessness, was what got me onto my feet on the board that very first lesson. I was never going to get very far with it, I recognised that, but that initial success was enough for me to persevere that summer. And then, even then, there was the feel of his firm hands on my wrists, my back, my calves. That, and having something new to learn, eased the grief for the dreams I was losing.

I don't know what to say and he's not helping. And it's up to him, it should be up to him: he's brought me here, back to the past, the past I've avoided. Then we both speak at once:

'You never…'

'Remember that night swim?'

And I'm silenced. Oh, yes, I remember that night swim.

It was here. Yanni and Luke were sixteen and I was eighteen, back for the summer after a year of college and living in a flat with another girl. I'd been to a beach party at Cylinder Beach, where friends of mine were staying in the camping ground. I'd caught the local bus to Point Lookout, Luke and Yanni allowed to come too, as long as I 'looked after' them. I'd been drinking Summer Wine and everything was dark except around the beach fire, and confusing. There were boys around me – sometime, somehow, I'd become someone to try to impress. Luke and Yanni had been drinking too – they'd got some beer from somewhere. And then they suddenly disappeared. I stood up from the boy who had progressed to leaning his shoulder against mine, and the other trying to talk to me, and I panicked. Luke and Yanni were my responsibility, after all. Someone said they'd headed off down the beach, so I ran in that direction.

And found them in the sea, in the cove – heard them first.

'Come in!' they whooped at me. Their clothes were strewn all over the place, even their jocks. 'Chicken!' Yanni called, and clucked and crowed.

They're crazy, I thought. Hadn't they seen *Jaws*? They were duck-diving and splashing and I caught a glimpse of white buttocks. What the hell, I thought. And pulled off my clothes, down to my knickers and bra.

And then all I remember is being in the sea, caught playfully around the waist under water by Yanni, his flesh a shock to me, the brief touch of his hardness on my leg enough to bring the blood to my face. And then diving under the water too, twisting away from him and surfacing, laughing, to the night sky – and feeling suddenly as if my life were starting all over again, as if I were reborn, baptised by moonlight, by the primary sea, by the warm night air and cool blackness of the water, and by the whirling, massive mystery of the stars.

'And after? Remember the day after?' His shoulder is touching mine and I can feel his rum breath on my cheek.

There was no surfing for Luke or me the next day. He felt as seedy as I did, I could tell. We both slept in.

Then my mother suggested a picnic at Blue Lake. My father wanted to paint it. I pleaded period pain, but Luke couldn't get out of going without confessing his hangover. Luke raised his eyes to the ceiling as he trundled after our parents and grandparents, past me lying on the couch.

I was nearly asleep again when Yanni turned up. My heart bumped against my ribs when I recognised him through my eyelashes.

'Luke around?' He'd come straight in the front door, which was as usual wide open.

'No,' I mumbled, half sitting up. 'They've all gone to Blue Lake.'

'Oh. Wanna come for a swim?' He wasn't looking at me but at a paperweight on the table just inside the door. He picked it up and turned it over.

'Uh – okay,' I said, guardedly.

He turned those brilliant eyes on my then and I could have swooned.

I put on a bikini and found a towel. We walked north along Amity beach, to where it fanned out into broad shallow lagoons. I was conscious of his height beside me and an uneasiness with him; we were like animals unsure of a new scent.

The sun was hot, prickling hot; when we got to the lagoons I spread my towel and knelt on it. I tied my hair into a chignon and pulled sunscreen from my beach bag.

'You want some of this?' I said.

He shook his head, not looking at me.

'Put some on my back?'

His hands were hot and rippled over my shoulders gently. I could feel his breath, faster than normal, on my neck. I shuddered with pleasure when his stroking hand touched my side.

We had to wade out far because the tide was out. There was a very clear line between the green shallow water and the dark blue channel all the way along the beach. The channel was treacherous – known for its strong currents and lurking sharks. But it was also known for its dolphins, which, when I came there as a little girl, used to come right into the shallower water and allow Shelley and me to touch them.

Yanni dived straight into the channel suddenly, into that cold, dark blue. 'Come in!' he yelled, suddenly exhilarated, just as he had the night before.

I hesitated. Then I followed him in: followed him where I hadn't had the courage to go before.

This time, we didn't touch each other. We didn't even talk. We flirted for a while with the channel's danger, diving under, swimming out a little way; then I swam back into the shallow, warm lagoons.

We walked back silently, not looking at each other. The hangover made the silence acceptable: made the whole situation a little unreal, and therefore acceptable. We both knew what was going on. Words couldn't have made it any clearer.

There was no car at my grandparents'; he came with me into the kitchen. I found an orange in the fridge, and bit the skin from the end of it and started sucking out the juice. Yanni watched me. I squeezed the rest of the juice into a glass and began buttering slices of bread with cheese spread.

'Are you hungry?' I said, over my shoulder, not looking at him. 'I'll make you a sandwich.'

But he didn't answer. In the glass of a painting, I watched him slouched against a cupboard between the kitchen and the lounge, his hands in his pockets and his brown legs covered in white hairs like soft, new shoots; and I imagined what was going on in his red board shorts: the red flute of his penis growing like an exotic orchid, the blond hairs curling away from it like leaves.

I went into the lounge room with the plate of sandwiches and some apples and brushed an elbow against his midriff as I passed him. He leapt as if my arm were on fire.

'Sorry!' I said, and felt hysterical giggles in my throat. I took an apple and carried it to the window, rubbing it against my thigh.

The silence went on. I began to eat the apple slowly and neatly. The street outside the overgrown fence shimmered gently. I heard a soft noise and then his hand on my shoulder was like an electric shock.

When I remember him, I see him with his eyelids slanted and sheened with desire. His chest was bare and hairless and his head was so blond it glowed like a halo in the shadows of my room. He leaned over me and when his lips closed on my mouth his breath was a poured-out sigh. As he moved, light through a blind angled across his skin and when his heart was pressed against my breast I felt it beat like the wings of a trapped bird.

I kissed his cheekbones and his eyelids, the parts of his face which make me want to cry. We dropped our clothes and our bodies slipped against each other in shivery, nervous leaps. On my body, his young limbs felt like another woman's, they were so soft...

And then, just before he came, he drew back and panted and his eyes were red with fear. Was it a religious hell he envisaged or my burden of love? Were both possible hells? Or was he just terrified of his own sexuality and the fear I saw was at the power of his own human flesh?

Then the fear closed under his eyelids and he came with shuddering, violent spasms; and when it was over he lay on me with his eyes closed and the heat from his body trickled down my skin.

He had taken me trembling with disbelief. And that, in part, was what made him so desirable, which drew me back again and again to him – his gratitude, his articulated disbelief at my allowing him to handle me, touch me, explore me with his penis and his hands and his mouth, at my compliance with any whispered fantasy. But of course that was only part of it: the other was that I knew, I felt I had known since I first felt the shock of his gaze, that it would happen. That he had power over me, despite his youth; that I would give him anything he asked for and take anything he offered.

Oh guilt, I felt some guilt. I had had a religious upbringing, after all. And embarrassment. Luke found out, of course. But above all, running in my veins like a fever, an obsessive, unnatural, blinding *hunger* for him.

I didn't know, afterwards, what he thought of me. He didn't speak. He lay beside me with his green, cool eyes watching. His cheeks were flushed and the skin of his forehead was sheened, like satin. I looked at his eyelashes, so dark, looked at their length, and I touched his bottom lip. He half-smiled and kissed my fingers with the smile.

I had a shower and when I came back he was dressed and the bed straightened. He had had no lunch and he was eating, absently, the apple I had started – and I didn't even notice the symbolism.

And I knew that I was in love with Yanni. Deeply, wholly. Obsessively. And I thought he loved me that way too.

My mother found out about us. Towards the end. When we'd become so close we were reckless. She caught us on the veranda of my grandmother's house, him lying on me with his hand under my skirt – his mother and father drinking cocktails with them to celebrate her birthday, Luke so embarrassed by us that he had strolled off to the beach – and she came out quietly, looking quietly for me, to ask if I, being eighteen, would like a cocktail too…

Careless.

I suddenly sensed her shadow, falling over us; her intake of breath. Then her shadow swinging abruptly, the click of her heels, fading. Just a note on my dresser, later. 'I hope to God you're using something.'

Well, she'd had so little to do with my life, even by then. She recognised that she could give me nothing I needed or wanted; I had moved out of her house into a flat and all she could do was throw up her hands and say she had done her bit, and that she must trust in the values she had instilled in me and I must make my own mistakes.

But I had him all that first summer – in a cave shaped like a breaking wave which no one else seemed to know about. I ignored him if I saw him with other people…partly, perhaps, because I could not bear to watch him weave his magic over others, and partly to preserve a sort of shivery delicious secrecy in our relationship; even when Peri came over to join me for two weeks, he and I still managed to meet. And then he came to my flat in Brisbane over six months the next year too, after school. He went to high school on the mainland, so I'd pick him up when we could arrange it. And we made love and smoked joints and talked on the soft cushions of sated desire. I knew of all his hopes, the extended pattern of his life dream, at least in terms of achievement… And we talked of painting and poetry, philosophy and psychology. He looked at my paintings and accepted the ones he liked, and he gave me in return little unexpected gifts – a shell bangle, translucent amber beads threaded into an anklet; once, a bizarrely beautiful dog whelk. Mutual gifts which, I believed, forged the first link in the chain of our lives to-gether… So romantic, I was! I believed in the continuity of things… but we both did – his dreams are strung like notes, dripped across the chords of my late childhood…at nights on the beach we watched the stars move across the sky and talked of the power of the universe and our own vague attempts to shape our destinies…

His arm has moved around my shoulder. 'We were like gods, weren't we?' he whispers. 'Untouchable. Outside morality. The world was ours to take.'

'We had everything,' I say.

Until then, that day. That last time, halfway through the year, when he held me so tenderly, and then told me he was leaving. With only the vague promise of return for me to cling to.

I crouch under his arm, then slowly lift my head. I stare at him and his eyes are heavy and soft, and I think, now. Now, I'll ask if he has come back for me, if this is why he is here. And I say, clearly, calmly, 'Why did you never contact me?' My heart thuds against my breast.

He keeps looking at me, but I can't read his eyes. He hesitates; then he drops his gaze. He says, 'I rang you.' Pauses. 'Before you got married.'

And, dimly, a memory surfaces…a phone call, a slurred, drunken voice calling me by my full first name, a name few people know, saying, 'Come on, you remember me'…music and voices in the background… and me saying, coldly, 'I'm sorry, I have no idea who you are, no idea' …then the connection abruptly broken. My puzzlement…and the voice so different I'd never once thought it might be him…

He flicks a glance at me. 'I wanted to stop you, or something…but I knew you were pregnant – Luke told me. So I…' He frowns and looks down again, then back at me. He hesitates. Then he raises his chin and looks over my head, out to sea, and when he speaks again his voice is stronger, resolute and abrupt: 'I'd just lost the surf heats in Bondi. I had nothing to offer you.'

And I feel his body, heavy and warm, wrapped around me, drawing me closer. I look up at his silver face and even though I'm choking, thinking, no, no, there was more than that, there's something you're not telling me still, I whisper, 'Why aren't you cold? You've hardly anything on…'

He smiles and I think the smile is a little sad. 'A bodysuit,' he says, 'under this thing.'

I thread my fingers through the black mesh and press them on his chest. It's slippery, satiny, like the sheer Lycra stockings I sometimes wear. I glance up at him again and his eyes are soft and cynical and sad.

'Can't let the image down.'

Then before I can speak, before I can pull him up and shake myself and say, no, no, I've distracted you, you're not getting away with it that easily, tell me the truth, tell me what happened, he lowers his face: and my mouth is warm and home and my body is wrapped about in his thin and lovely and broken wings.

7

He's holding me, cradling me, and the strength and bulk of his arms is foreign but startlingly real. The wind from the sea lifts his fringe as he raises his face from mine. I can feel the imprint of his shoulder's black mesh on my cheek and the vibration of his heart against his skin.

Don't speak, I think: don't speak. I don't want to talk. Not now. What do reasons matter? I only want him to kiss me again, to drown me – I have a wild urge to say, I love you, Yanni, I love you, I always have, I can't help it, take me here on the sand before I can think about it, before I can make a rational decision, sweep me off my feet, take me, fuck me, take the decision from me, make it yours, make it quick and clean like a knife so I know where one life ends and another begins, make it a realised fantasy but nothing to do with real life, fuck me and love me and ask nothing more of me and none of them can touch us, it will be our own paradise and we can do it like walking through a wall into another world…

But he is looking at me and his eyes are tender and dreamy and luminous and his lips are parted to speak –

'You!'

The voice is slurred, coming from behind us, from the top of the sand dune. Both of us jump, turning simultaneously – and there's Mick, swaying gently, a beer can in his hand, his face heavy and twisted in the moon-shadowed trees.

'Mighta known it'd be you. You, ya fuckin' bastard. Get all the bloody chicks. Fuckin' prick!'

He flings the beer can suddenly, but it's empty and falls wide of Yanni. He comes towards us, out from under the casuarinas, and I can see his eyes are crazy, wide-set and glazed.

We're on our feet, Yanni with his arm still around me.

'It's not how you think!' I can't help it; I have to butt in because Mick, wild-eyed, is stumbling toward Yanni. 'I've just known Yanni for so long – ages. He was my –'

'Fuckin' prick!' He hasn't even heard me; his eyes are focused at last and he lunges at Yanni, who flings me away from him just before the impact.

'Stop it!' I scream – I'm appalled – this stupid surfie yobbo thinking he has any sort of claim on me and fighting over his claim, as if I'm something he can own –

And then I stand quite still and their stupid struggle goes on silently as if it's in a film I'm watching, and I think, of course I am owned. By Mark, by my children... I begin to back away, watching them, watching Yanni gain the upper hand because Mick is far too drunk to coordinate his fists – then I turn and scramble up the sand dune and find the opening to the track.

I'm appalled, I'm appalled. Not at Mick any more, but at myself. At what I wanted – was allowing – to happen. What if we really had – what if Mick had turned up fifteen minutes later, and it got back to Peri, who wouldn't understand, wouldn't understand any of it, or it got back to Mark, whose reaction could be God knows how unpredictable – what if we hadn't used protection and I could be pregnant or if Yanni had some sort of horrible disease...

Then Mick's howl comes back to me in my head. 'Ya fuckin' bastard. Get all the bloody chicks.' And I'm appalled again at myself. I don't know him. Not any more – not this adult Yanni. Who is he? What has he become? Am I just another woman to him now, another score for his board, another 'chick' to be won, like something in a raffle?

But how could I ever be anything else? When I am married; when my children's happiness – and, despite everything, despite Mark's obsession with his work and his destructive jealousies and the simmering hostility we each feel for the other at depressingly regular intervals, Mark's happiness too, I know – was all tied up with Mark and me staying together? So how could I allow any development with Yanni, even if he wanted it? All we could ever have between us was sex – and clandestine sex at that.

Yanni could do it. Look how he finished with me eleven years ago. Probably did it all the time. Probably had no intention of anything else with me.

But could I? Could I have sex with Yanni now without wanting to own him?

I'm nearly through to the road. I'm almost running, striding fast, panting.

The full implication of what almost happened has risen like hangover remorse. It's the guilt and self-reproach I felt once when I almost had a car accident; it's a shame of my own humanity.

I don't walk along the road, the shortest way back to the party, the way Yanni would expect me to go if he was coming after me. I weave through the trees to Cylinder Beach, then cut in to the road when I can hear music. And by then my panic has settled a little, and I am thinking more rationally.

I approach the party cautiously. It's still raging, and I stand on the edge of the light, scanning bodies and faces for Peri. I just want to find her and get out of there. I'm jumpy, nervous that Yanni will be back before I can get away; I don't want to – can't – face him again until I've had time to think. To look at everything from different angles; to turn the crystal and see how he sees me, how Peri sees him…and Haden.

And I'm struck with guilt again. I'd forgotten about Haden. About where he might have taken Peri. About deserting the party – deserting her, if she's come back.

But I can't find Peri anywhere, and Yanni doesn't turn up either. And eventually I'm too jittery to wait any longer, and I head off across Cylinder Beach again; and in the waning moonlight trek over the sand to the rocks and climb up the cliff to the pub, to my silver Laser standing quite alone in the car park, glimmering coldly and serenely under the darkened heavens.

There's another car – a sleek, gold-glinting sporty one whose make I don't recognise – parked outside Peri's place. The moon has slipped close to the horizon, so I can barely see the path leading down to the house, which is in blackness. I shuffle through papers in the glovebox to find the torch Peri and I brought with us when we left; with the help of that, I follow the track down the side of the house and up the back steps to the deck. To my relief, the French door is unlocked; I slip inside silently, lock the door behind me, and switch off the torch.

My eyes adjust slowly to the interior. There is moonlight filtering through tree shadows: I make out Judy's bulk on the couch, and can hear her gentle rhythmic breathing. I'm aware of the ticking of a clock. To my left is the half-ajar door to the children. Then to my right, in my peripheral vision, I see something move.

I start. I stare into the darkness, beyond the dappled moonlight on the polished floor, and at first I see nothing. Then gradually a black shape takes form. Standing on the lower steps of the internal staircase is a man in a long black coat.

I shrink back against the door, my heart in my throat. But I know who it is, of course I know who it is: Haden – I recognised his car, and now the coat, it has to be – and I have no reason to fear Haden – if anything, he is my host…but nevertheless, I can't seem to steady my pulse.

He descends the last steps, his footfalls surprisingly soft on the timber. He moves across the floor into the moonlight, and shadows ripple like water across one side of his face: I make out an angular nose, a prominent cleft chin, a fall of shaggy black hair. He seems massive… his body seems to carry a weight of power that is mesmerising…and I see that he is holding something – something curious, whose shape I can't quite make out. Then he shoves whatever it is into one of his pockets, and gestures to me.

He turns and crosses to the stairs again, and begins to ascend.

His meaning is unmistakable. I hesitate, then follow.

It is blind black once I turn the bend in the stairs which cuts out the faint moonlight below, and I stumble, and grope with my hands – and stifle a shriek when my fingers grasp prickly wool. Then my cold hand is caught in a warm, powerful one, and I regain my footing, and he leads me, surprisingly gently, through the darkness up the next flight, then along the corridor and through a doorway, although into which of the upstairs rooms I have no idea.

He releases my hand, and I stand still, disoriented. Then there is a triangle of grey fretted light, and I see he has looped back a curtain, and that we are on the western side of the house, with the setting moon glimmering her last beams onto the brocade covering of a single bed.

He sinks down onto the bed, and again gestures to me. I perch on the edge of the mattress.

When he speaks, his voice is pleasant and surprisingly cultured, but there is an edge of impatience to it: and the words are very clear despite the low pitch of their volume. 'I'm sorry. I hope I didn't startle you. I just wanted to have a word with you before I leave.'

'I…no, it's okay. It's…Haden, isn't it?'

'Mm.' The word is clipped, restless. 'And you are Peri's cousin.'

'Ven.'

'Yes.'

I wait, expectantly. He has such a powerful presence, such an aura of assertion, that I feel no need to say any more. But the silence goes on.

Then, just when I think, oh no, he's waiting, he's expecting something from me, and I begin to search frantically for whatever he might have to reproach me, he abruptly stands up, turning away, and shuffles his fingers through his hair, so it spikes up in his profiled silhouette, and he mutters, 'I… Oh, look it doesn't matter.'

I swallow, shaking my head, with the same feeling I used to get when my father was about to reprimand me for some misdeed I hadn't known I'd committed. 'If it's about taking Peri away from the party –'

'I wanted to ask you a favour.'

We have spoken simultaneously.

'Sure, sure, ask away.' My voice is hurried and a bit breathless. I am suddenly conscious of the fact that he is not in the least aware of my discomfort.

'It's about…Yanni.'

I blink, and take a breath. 'Yanni?'

'You know him.' It's not a question.

I nod. The faint light is behind him and he's turned to face me again, so I can't see his expression, only a black cut-out with hair ruffled and spiked; but he can probably make out mine, which I'm sure is guarded.

'We're old friends. I've known him since we were children.'

'Yes. I watched you at the party. It was obvious you knew him well.'

I jerk my head up. I thought I had been discreet…

'And he…and Peri?' The question is almost snapped.

'I…' I don't know what to say, what exactly he's asking me. 'Yanni and Peri? I don't…well, no, no, I mean they're not…they haven't…'

A snort. 'No. I didn't think so. Not yet, anyway.'

I stare at the silhouette of tossing head against the triangle of faint light. Not yet? I think. But not ever… Yanni has come back for me – he made that clear, tonight, surely, didn't he? Despite everything – Mick's comment – he has come back for me…

'And anyway, his type never stay with one woman for long.'

My intake of breath is audible. His type?

'Well, then. I'll let you get to bed now.' He shoves his hands in his pockets abruptly, and moves toward the door.

'I…'

He pauses and looks around at me, and I can see him visibly checking his impatience. 'Yes?'

'Peri is back, isn't she?'

'Yes, of course.'

'Oh, okay. Good.' I hesitate: I want to say more, to ask him what is going on with her, between them, but he just stands there in silence, waiting, and I lose my nerve. 'That – was all. Good night, then.'

'Yes. You too. We'll meet again, I'm sure.' Then he makes a curious gesture, almost a half bow – and the object in his pocket protrudes, and I see what it is.

A paintbrush.

I use the torch I'm still clutching to pick my way back down the stairs. My brain is fuddled. Don't even try, I think. Leave it till tomorrow.

I find my bedroom; I strip off my clothes and sink with overwhelming fatigue into the bed beside Charlotte. I lie still for one moment, wide-eyed in the darkness; then I surrender to the weariness of my body, and the gradually calming ticking of my brain, and the murmur of my children's steady, quiet and trusting breath.

There are bands of light across my eyes and Charlotte's high, piping voice comes from somewhere distant. It takes me a moment to wade through the bleariness behind my forehead to unstick my eyelids and read my watch. Six a.m. – not enough, not nearly enough sleep.

I can hear Ross's deeper timbre too, then what must be Judy's comforting drone. They're down on the beach, by the sound of it. I sigh with relief and lie back with my eyes shut, pushing the rising memories from last night under the blanket of subconsciousness.

I'm just dozing off again when a knock on the door makes me jump. I open my eyes to Peri standing quietly in the doorway, looking at me.

'Oh, you got back safely, then.' My voice is croaky. 'Morning.'

But she doesn't reply: she just stands there, looking frail and thin in a loose jumper with her hands in her jeans pockets.

I groan and rub my eyes and struggle to sit up, pulling the warm bedclothes with me because I'm dressed in a thin cotton nightdress. 'I saw you go off with…some guy in the long black coat. I waited for you to come back, but…' I trail off, pulling the doona up more firmly and loosening my hair so it can fall warmly over my shoulders.

She comes slowly over to the bed. 'I went back. But you were gone. So was Yanni. People said you left together.' She stands at the end of the bed. Her mouth is a straight line. Her face without make-up has a smatter of freckles and her black hair is pulled untidily into a band.

'Oh,' I say. I take a breath and make my voice careless. 'We went for a walk. It was so noisy there – and Yanni and I used to be great friends... You'd gone – I didn't know what was going on.' I look at her steadily then. 'Yanni said the man you went with was Haden? Your landlord?' With relief, I watch her lips pucker and her eyelids drop. I seize the advantage. 'I was worried about you – you left without saying anything – and Yanni was worried too.'

She raises her eyes and an eyebrow then. 'Why would Yanni be worried?' But there is a catch of interest beneath the skepticism.

'Well...' I twist one length of hair down my shoulder and arm and stare at the doona cover for inspiration. But all I can come up with is the truth. 'He said he didn't like Haden much.'

'Ah.' One side of her mouth twitches then. 'Not too many people do.'

'So...why did you go off with him?'

She sinks down onto the edge of the bed then. She curls her fingers in her lap and rubs them. 'He's – heard from Mum. God knows how she found out, but she knows he's letting me live here rent-free. She's furious, apparently. Wants him to kick me out. But she can't do anything. I'm quite old enough to make my own decisions. He told me I can stay here as long as I like.' She throws up her head as she says the last.

I'm silent. After a moment I say, 'So he dropped you back here last night? When you couldn't find me?'

'Mmm.'

I stare at her, but she won't meet my eye.

'And...he stayed for a while?'

She looks at me, then shifts her gaze, her face colouring slightly.

I take the plunge. 'Peri...I saw him. He spoke to me. It was late...'

'What did he tell you?' Her voice is so sharp she startles me.

I hesitate. 'Well...he didn't...he wanted to know if there is anything between you and Yanni.' I stare at her, and feel the muscles in my face tense. 'I don't know why he would expect me to know...'

She's looking at me fully, but I can't read her expression. After a moment, she says, 'So you would have told him that, obviously?'

'I – told him no. Well, you said the other night there wasn't...' I peter out. 'But Peri – what's it to Haden?'

Her eyes look wide and very dark: she twists her fingers in her lap again. She goes to speak, then closes her lips. Then she says, 'What did you think of Haden?' Her voice is curious.

'Well...I could hardly see him, it was so black. But I liked his voice: it was...sort of refined...could be very seductive, I imagine! And...he looked a bit vulnerable: he kept ruffling his hair, like some mad professor...' I grin then, and am relieved to see her face at last relax.

'He's not that bad, you know. He's kind – considerate. I've learnt a lot about him since I started living here – he drops in sometimes. And there are things he's told me about his past that sort of explain... I know a lot of people don't trust him, but he's been really good to me. Loves my paintings. Not many men do.'

'Oh,' I say.

'Don't look at me like that!'

'Like what?' I raise my eyebrows. Then I take a risk. 'Are you sure it's Yanni you're keen on over here?'

'Why?' She shoves a sleeve of her jumper up one wrist – a gesture I remember from when we were children – she's flared! Bad risk, I think.

'Sorry! Just teasing. But he is a good catch – good looking, rich, obviously pretty taken with you...'

'And Yanni's just a has-been surfer?'

And the most beautiful man I have ever met. I shrug. 'Something like that.' Oh, treachery, I think. I don't meet her eye. 'Tell me more about Haden,' I say quickly. 'About his past?'

She glances at me. She goes quiet, thinking. Then she says, lifting her shoulders, 'Oh, stuff about his mother. How she was always palming him off to boarding schools – from the time he was eight. Eight! Two years older than Ross.'

'Maybe she had to. There's only the one primary school here, and if she wanted private education for him...'

'It wasn't just that.' She frowning now and her hands are a little agitated and suddenly I'm staring at her wrist, the one she's pushed the sleeve away from… 'She did love him, he says, but she was always too busy for him. She used to run this guesthouse – quaint name, isn't it? But that's what it was called. His father wasn't around much, I gather, and she needed the money. And he was an only child – he was often lonely, at boarding school and when he was here on holidays…we have some things in common…'

But I'm not listening: I'm transfixed by a red bruise that encircles her wrist like a bracelet.

'She died, from cancer. When he was sixteen. He told me one night that sometimes he cries for her in his sleep. Don't you think that's sad? I think that's why he's so patient with Mum. But why he likes me defying her too! But, the trouble is, he's sort of…possessive. Well, of course, you know that, don't you, from what he said to you last night. And manipulative. He's very good at getting his own way. And that – well, scares me a little.'

I'm silent. I'm trying to make sense of her innuendo and its connection to the bruise. Oh, Peri, I think: what have you got yourself into?

''Cause I do like Yanni. Heaps. Oh, I don't know.' She gives her shoulders a sudden shake, and her sleeve slips down over her wrist again. 'Maybe you should meet Haden properly? Give me your opinion? I'll ring him, see if he…'

But before she or I can say anything more, through the closed door we hear the muffled ringing of the telephone in the kitchen. Peri starts, then springs up, her face curiously alight; and I think, oh God which does she think it is: Yanni or Haden?

But I don't have time to think that through, because she immediately calls, 'Venny! It's for you – the mainland.'

I stare blankly for a second, then push back the doona and hurry out to the kitchen.

'Ven?' The voice is clipped, abrupt. I don't recognise it.

'Yes?'

'It's Zac.'

Of course. Zac works in Mark's furniture factory. 'Mark's had an accident. Not too serious, but I'm taking him to the hospital. Thought you should know. Got your number out of him.'

'What – what's he –'

'Nothing too bad. Cut his leg. Nothing too serious. Just thought you should know.'

'I'll come back now – on the next ferry – what hospital?'

'Mater.'

'Okay. Tell him we'll come straight away.'

'Right.'

There's a click and the line is dead.

8

'How did it happen?'

We're driving from the Mater Hospital along Wynnum Road. The sky is bright blue and cloudless; a south-westerly sprang up as we were coming across the bay on the ferry. The radio is on Mark's favourite station. The horizon is clear and airy Mozart flows over us, but the atmosphere in the car is still sticky.

'I caught two fish, Dad – Mum's going to cook them for lunch! Judy showed me how to gut them.'

Ross seems almost to be speaking to himself: when I glance in the rear-view mirror at him his eyes are focused dreamily out the window. Charlotte is quiet, sucking her thumb.

There was no time to find out details at the hospital.

Mark was edgy, impatient. 'Let's get out of here,' he said as soon as we found him in an orange plastic chair in outpatients. In his black beard, his lips had closed firmly over those words, and his eyes had been challenging steel. There were rusty streaks on his grey shorts and faded navy sweater. His left leg was bandaged from knee to thigh.

'Circular saw.'

I wince.

'Trying to get those chairs finished. Behind with them. It was stupid – I had the bloody stump wedged against my thigh trying to cut the bastard straight.' He's staring through the windscreen. 'Nearly had it right, too.'

'How many stitches?'

'I dunno. Five, six.'

Twelve, the hospital told me when I rang from Cleveland. He was lucky not to slice a major nerve.

'Does it hurt?'

'Bit. It was numb to start with. Blood everywhere. Zac gave me a lift to the hospital. You have a good time?' He glances abruptly at me.

We had a fight before I went away; he is still wary of me although all my defences are down.

'Mmm. Lovely. It was great.'

'How's Peri?'

'Oh, fine. Still drinking like a fish.' I bite my lip. He disapproves of her already, and that will just fuel his prejudice. But when I flick a look at him, I see he has turned back to the windscreen, hardly listening. His beard masks his expression.

'You shouldn't have come back. Don't know what you thought was going to happen to me.'

I shrug and glance at him again. He has narrowed his eyes against the light.

'What'd they give you for the pain?'

'Just a local. And some codeine, for when it wears off.' His eyelids close.

We're approaching the turn-off for our street: but there are shops further along Wynnum Road.

'Pick up some things – milk and bread?'

'Mmm. And a chicken or something for lunch.' He settles back in the bucket seat, still with his eyes closed. His face looks impermeable, forbidding.

'What about my fish?' Ross's voice is a sudden wail.

'Oh, darling, of course we'll cook your fish.' Guilt-stricken, I catch his eye in the rear-view mirror. 'Dad probably just didn't hear you – his leg's very sore, you know – wait until he sees how big the fish are!'

Ross sits back, semi-mollified. It's unusual for Mark not to praise Ross for things Ross is obviously proud of, but it's not unusual for him to be negative to everyone when he's tense with me.

I pick up the milk and bread and some more codeine. The children trundle up the stairs that are cut into a rock wall leading to our front yard, then up wooden steps that land us on our Queenslander's veranda. Mark limps after them, carrying the food.

I unpack the car, unpack the bags and prepare the fish. Mark turns on the television and I turn on the bath. I wash the salt from the children's skin, get them dressed and cook lunch. The children chatter and Mark eats and I feel drained, as if someone has pulled the plug and drawn the life out of me. It's partly the after-effect of a late night, but there is more to it as well. More than I'll admit.

In the night, I dream again of Yanni. I dream I'm standing watching him writing in a book. I keep asking him questions about the book, but his answers are all confused or confusing. Eventually, I lie down on the bed in the room; he lies beside me. Then softly, deliberately, he moves his face to my still-speaking one and places his mouth over mine. I feel his lips, his tongue move into my mouth; my body is transfixed with desire and a warm, intense sighing, like a climax, of something, at last, reaching culmination.

I wake, and look over at Mark. His back is to me and dappled moonlight plays on his bare skin. His bandaged thigh rests above the blankets. I pull the doona up around his back. The night air blowing in the open French doors is cold.

I touch his neck. His skin is damp; his temperature is still up. I roll onto my back and stare at the shadows moving like moths on the wall.

If Mark could only bring things out into the open! But little things throw him into a black mood: and then it's as if he's in a self-sealing envelope; even when he wants to come out, he has to use strategies against his own defences to release himself. I certainly can only let him out by tearing, and then using my own strategies of protection. I can't pin it down; I can't work out when it all started, when we lost our closeness, how we fell into our pattern of rage and resentment...but it was after the children were born, certainly... And then it occurs to me that maybe it was because the children became the focus of my world, instead of him, and work became the focus of his, instead of me...but work doesn't love you back, as children do...

If he's better in the morning, he will go to work again. He's behind with an order for chairs made from varnished branches and slabs of tree trunk and iron filigree: one of his favourite designs. I'll take Ross to school and entertain Charlotte and clean the house and cook and garden. In the evening, Mark will get home around six and we'll eat and I'll help Ross with his homework and read the children a story each; then I'll iron while Mark and I watch television and at ten we'll go to bed. We won't make love; we rarely do unless we've been out drinking, and now there's of course his thigh and bad mood to consider as well.

If he's not better, he'll spend the day in bed. I'll bring him paracetamol, or codeine, and things to eat and drink; and he'll sleep and grunt at me and I'll do all the things I would have done anyway.

The night feels cold and desolate. I get out of bed and wrap a gown around me. I go out onto the veranda outside our bedroom.

We live in a timber house at almost the top of a hill, a few kilometres as the crow flies from the city. The bedroom veranda faces the road and a sweep of suburban valley; to the right, obscured by trees, are the city lights.

The night air is still. The south-westerly has lulled, leaving the city chilled. There are two tall gum trees and a silky oak in the front yard. In the darkness, the trees look like frozen fountains or petrified shadows. I stare at them and at the black and white neat houses which stretch in rows to the river. That's it, I think, that's what my life is like. A black and white frozen panorama: no colour or passion…

I shake myself. Stop being so bloody self-pitying, I think. Stop it. Go back to bed. It's just seeing Yanni again, feeling attractive, wanted, remembering all that love, that sex. That excitement –

With no possibility of seeing him again. No point. The moment lost.

Depression settles again.

I think about Peri. Her relationship with Haden shifts uncomfortably forward, from its stored place at the back of my brain. What is Haden really like? I think of what Yanni said, about him perhaps being involved in drug dealing, about Peri's story about his childhood, about the bruise on Peri's wrist. The bruise particularly worries me. It seems out of place somehow... Peri wasn't angry with him, as I would expect her to be if he had deliberately hurt her – in fact, quite the opposite: she was defensive of him. And why did he have a paintbrush in his pocket? I shake my head. I have to ring her, I think.

Then I'm back to thinking about Yanni again. And face the fact that he is attracted to Peri. She is attractive to two men. What excitement, I think, what a thrill the shifting landscape of her future must hold! And I'm suddenly not just jealous of the fact that Yanni might want her – I am envious, startlingly envious, of the possibility that love might transform her life, fill it out, make it whole. Enrich it, sustain it, make it flower. A two-sided love, mutually supportive and affirmative – but with room to breathe and with a central, dark, fierce, fusing of spirit...

Like the love I had, once, with Yanni.

And with Mark?

I sigh.

The world outside is very still and cold. A train whistle echoes from somewhere across the dark river, and I have a wrench of loneliness that is like a physical spasm. I shake myself and try to reason that I feel this way because Mark is angry with me, and because of the dream I had earlier about Yanni, and because of the coldness of the winter night. I try to reason that when Mark and I have made up and I stop dredging up memories of old love and I am warm and well-rested things will be all right...

But when I wake in the morning, the heaviness is still there, together with a dread of the day like an old, old dread I remember with despair from somewhere in my childhood.

And Mark is no better. He's sleeping when I wake but his cheeks are flushed. I push the doona off him and touch his forehead but he doesn't stir. His body emits a feverish, uncomfortable heat. I feel ashamed of my dream and of my midnight resentment, but I feel heavy and sad too.

The children are up and playing a make-believe game in their bedroom.

'I'm the emperor,' I hear Ross say majestically, 'and you're just a slave.'

'What do you want me to do, Master?' says Charlotte in a subservient American accent.

It's only six-thirty. I draw open the curtains and unhook the French doors I opened last night and pull them shut tightly. The wind has freshened again. The air is clear and the sky too blue, like an artificial smile. The badly fitting doors whistle like yacht stays.

I pull on a tracksuit and the children hear me and come racing in. 'Shh!' I say. 'Daddy's sick. You've got to be very quiet now.'

They play the game, creeping out with me to the bathroom. But as soon as we are out of the bedroom, Charlotte tells me in her piping, excited voice about the game they've been playing; Ross contradicts her halfway through – Charlotte screams in frustration. I sit on the toilet and watch them, heavy-lidded. Broken sleep always makes my eyes harsh, as if my eyelids have a lining of sandpaper. Broken sleep, and depression.

I make toast and tea, boil eggs. The children chase each other around me, Ross teasing unbearably. The lino tiles are cold: their feet are pink around the edges.

'Put on your slippers!' I say. 'Why do you think you have them?'

'But I like the rabbit ones!' howls Charlotte, excited by the teasing.

'They're too small for you,' I say wearily.

'But I love them!'

'I don't need slippers,' says Ross defiantly.

'Okay, fine.' I turn back to the toaster. 'Just don't put your cold feet on me – or Daddy!'

But it's too late. Ross is chasing Charlotte down the hallway and I wince as I hear them land on the bed. There is a shriek, then another howl from Charlotte. I run in as a leaden-faced Mark is raising his palm to Ross's squirming bottom.

'Don't you dare!' I cry.

There's a silence, into which both the children begin to whimper. 'Get them out of here,' says Mark then, slowly easing his fingers from Ross's arm.

I glare at him. 'They don't understand,' I say. My anger is a tight fist in my throat. 'They just wanted to play.'

'Get them out of here.'

I take Ross to school at last and by nine o'clock Charlotte is settled in front of *Sesame Street*. I survey the littered plates, spilt milk and sugar, dredged toys like tidemarks, and remember my blood sugar is low because my tea didn't have any and that this depression might ease if I eat something.

I spoon yoghurt over muesli, and take some with tea and milk in to Mark. He's asleep again, and his forehead is still hot. I leave the breakfast and some codeine on the table beside the bed. I eat my breakfast at the kitchen table, watching through western windows the cold wind glitter the leaves of a gum tree. Then I make the children's beds, wash the dishes, sweep the floor, tidy the toys and load the washing machine. When I look in on Mark again the tea and food and tablets are gone, and his forehead is cool.

By the evening, Mark is up and about, but not speaking to me. He cannot bear me undermining his authority. That, on top of the argument we had before I went to stay with Peri, has triggered his hostility again. Cold War 150. I go through the mechanics of preparing dinner and tidying up and bathing the children and reading them stories, and Mark eats without a word to me, limps over to the television, and stays there until long after I have gone to bed.

9

At six in the morning, I wake with a start to the phone ringing. Mark glares at me through half-open lids as if it's my fault. It stops.

Then Ross calls from the kitchen, 'It's for you, Mum!'

Mark rolls over, case dismissed.

I pull on a wrap and stumble blearily to the kitchen. We have only one phone.

'Hello?'

'Ven. My Venus.' The voice is slurred, drunken. I want to gasp; my heart begins to hurt as if it has been thumped.

'Yanni.' My voice is a whisper.

'The very one. Well done. Well done. Never thought you'd guess.'

'But I – how did you – where are you?' I feel frightened by the urgency of my heart.

There is a violent clatter at the other end, then his voice lurches back. 'Still a beautiful bum. Beautiful. Exactly the same. Eternal youth – what's your secret? Come over. Come on now.' His voice is softer, the slur draining from it; he could almost be pleading.

But it's not making sense – he's not making sense. I shake my head, frowning at the wall, at its calendar print of two little girls picking flowers in a bright European field. 'Yanni, are you drunk? Where are you?'

There is music playing in the background: I know who it is instinctively, before I hear the unmistakable surging voice: 'When I listen to your heart I hear the whole world turning / I see the shooting stars falling through your trembling hands…' The music Yanni and I made love to, in the car, in the dark, in the past: music clothed in memories as tangible as silk.

'Yanni?'

There is a clatter and the phone cuts out. I hold the receiver, which beeps insistently to be replaced, and lean my other hand against the wall. It is six o'clock in the morning and Yanni has been out all night from the sound of it, and if I knew where he was and if I were a free woman, I would not hesitate to pull on the first thing I could find and drive to wherever he was.

But I don't know where he is and I am not a free woman.

Mark is tight-lipped when he comes into the kitchen later. He's dressed for work, overalls covering his cut leg and vulnerability. I wonder for a minute whether he overheard my conversation, but the kitchen is a long way from the bedroom. He doesn't even ask me who it was. He doesn't look at me. He pours tea from the pot I've made and gets his breakfast.

The mad morning starts. While I make toast and dole out cereal, I try to cajole Ross into dressing for school; he is absorbed in building something with Lego in his room across the hall from the kitchen and won't be distracted. Then Charlotte tries to help him with his construction, and crashes the whole thing down. Screams and tearing cries. I burn the toast trying to separate them. Mark speaks to no one and sits at the table eating his two courses doggedly. Charlotte's cries turn to sniffles on my shoulder; Ross refuses breakfast. I spoon Weetbix into Charlotte's mouth with her still on my hip. Ross eventually dresses and eats peanut butter on toast; we pile into the car with library books, sports shoes and homework at a quarter to nine.

And peace descends with the front door closed on the wind and with the *Play School* anthem at nine-thirty.

Then the phone rings again.

And this time I am awake enough for my heart to leap to my throat with possibility. Or maybe intuition.

I let it ring four times, staring at it. Then I pick it up.

'Hello? Venny speaking,' I say, formally.

'Ven. It's Yanni.'

'Yes.'

'Can I see you? Do you want to see me?' His voice is subdued and thick. He sounds as if he's in bed, just woken. I hear him drinking. The room behind him is quiet.

'Yes.'

'Okay. Look. I have to get some sleep. Only had a couple of hours. Meet me tomorrow? Kodak Beach at Southbank?'

I think quickly. I normally work Wednesday afternoons at an art supply shop in the city. I can drop Charlotte to her usual day care early, and let the shop know I'll be late. 'All right. Eleven-thirty?'

'Okay.' The word is a breathy sigh.

I wash the dishes and dry them. The sink is below a broad window which views the back deck to the right and the city to the left; I keep stopping the job to stare out at the city. The winter light outside is cold and bright, with clean, elegant lines because the wind has whipped the smog away; the trees all the way to the river bob and sway and the city skyscrapers beyond New Farm Park look as if they've been outlined in charcoal. He's out there somewhere, I think. Out there, in one of the houses in this vast city, in bed, thinking of me. In which building? In whose room?

I make the beds. On the wall behind mine, among paintings and other framed poems, is a copy of e.e. cummings's 'since feeling is first'. I read it, distractedly. I turn on the washing machine and pull out the vacuum cleaner, but I keep returning to the kitchen to look out of the window, and to my room to look at the poem. In the end, I leave the washing and the vacuuming and the children's jumbled mess. I wheel out Charlotte's stroller and rug us both up and we go out.

I walk down to a park by the river, pushing a chattering, blossom-cheeked Charlotte. The poincianas and jacarandas are bare, their twigs casting frail shadows. The river is brown and heavy, inscrutable. Charlotte jumps out of the stroller and runs in the wind, the cold forgotten, to all her favourite climbing frames. I sit on the bench and subdue the agitation that flutters like feathers in my chest, and force myself, for the first time in full consciousness, to open the box of frightening, fragile possibilities I have held in my heart since Peri first uttered Yanni's name.

So, possibility number one. A possibility I have to face. Yanni has come back to the island because he loves it, not me. He loves the life there. Nowhere else has measured up. I have nothing to do with his coming back: his running in to me by chance has made him want to catch up on old times... But I shake my head. No. He realises that I still want him, even after all these years, and he still wants me – if he were only being friendly, why that kiss? Why that drunken phone call? But even so, maybe it's just that he was flattered and sexually keyed and he rang me because he wants to have a simple affair with me.

Again. Only the last 'affair' wasn't simple and this one wouldn't be either. The last was a culmination of years of unspoken sexual tension, Yanni's emergence into manhood, my realisation of my sexual power: and it was broken off because he was too young? Because he needed to experience the world, work out what he really wanted, go to Sydney, try out for the surf trials, spread his wings, be free, find his place in the world? Which might or might not be with me? These were the reasons I turned over and over in my head, trying to be rational, when I was nineteen and I knew what we had had to end...

Then suddenly I remember what he said to me on the beach when I asked him why he hadn't ever contacted me since. 'I wanted to stop you, or something...but I knew you were pregnant – Luke told me.'

So perhaps he had thought about me, sometimes...but he thought I was in love with Mark? I had decided to have children with Mark? Which was not the case – the pregnancy had been unplanned, an acci-dent...but something which I never considered terminating...I had fan-tasised about bringing up the child on my own, something I thought I would be happy to do at the time...a child would forever disperse the insecurity I felt about my place in the world, would be someone I could love unconditionally, and who would love me back, so...

But I baulk. I shake my head, a shivery, quick movement. That is treacherous, I think. Because I was in love with Mark then. I was. Yanni was always in some depth in my mind – he would surface in regular dreams – but I was in love with Mark, too. He was artistic, clever, beautiful in a blue, intense-eyed way... I shut my own eyes. I was in love with him. I was.

I met him at an art college party. Mark was postgraduate; I was in second year. He, like I, was older than his cohort. I, restless after Yanni went to Sydney, had dropped out of college and found a job and saved to go to Europe, only returning to college two years later. Mark had come to college as an adult student. He had worked as a welder for some years, and that gave him the edge in an area of sculpture. Being practical, he saw a niche market in sculptured timber and ironworked furniture...that is still his speciality.

But of course I knew none of that when I met him. He was a tall, clean-shaven man intently in conversation with a balding lecturer when I first saw him. I was dancing with a short and lecherous poet, who had somehow wormed his way into the party and my interest, but whose ego was beginning to bore me. After I had shoved with accentuated vigour his thrice-roaming hand from one of my buttocks, I catapulted into Mark.

He spilt wine into my hair and a blue stare into my face...his eyes were just like the angelic ones in the doll I had carted from home to home, from town to town, when I was a child – and his strong arm had automatically caught me around the ribs, to steady me. He touched, by accident, one of my breasts, too...and I watched heat flush across his face in the same way it was flushing across my body. I smiled.

I got him a drink, to replace the one I'd knocked. He talked warily to me to start with...he thought I was a bit of a hippie, he told me later. It is true that I dressed then in the accepted artist's uniform of loose cotton trousers and cheesecloth blouses: but I had no allegiance to anything political. I was an innocent, in many ways, I suppose – protected by the shell of my own refusal to engage in any depth with the outside world.

When I told him my name, and he asked if I was related to my father, whose name was known in those circles at the time, he seemed unimpressed with my answer. Instead, he did something which endeared him to me. He told me, suddenly, after staring at a couple who had started to pogo in the dangerously candlelit lounge room, that he had seen one of my paintings in the end-of-semester student exhibition, and that it had impressed him.

There was something about him that reminded me of my father. And he was like my father in the sense that he was a fine and dedicated artist and artisan; and he was well respected by his peers, as my father was. But there were differences, too, that were important differences from my father. My father was flamboyant at times, and loud and rude and passionate – as a young child, I had been frightened many times by his loud voice, raised in rage or in zeal. In comparison, in that early time of my knowing him, Mark was outgoing, but without my father's brashness; passionate about his work, but not to the point of rudeness… We drank a lot of wine together, in the early days, and he tended to be exuberant, perhaps, on that, and perhaps also my attention to him…

I didn't realise then that he was actually also quietly intense, with subterranean obsession. It had taken a long time for that intensity to resume a totally inner focus. I watched his attention to me fade, gradually, over the years. I suppose he thought, as my father certainly did, that women with children were bad conversationalists. His own father had died of a heart attack when Mark was in his early twenties, and my father definitely influenced him in his attitude to me, and women in general. We saw, and still see a lot of my parents. I have often wondered, as I've watched Mark and my father together, a glass of beer at each elbow, their heads locked together in profile across a table while my mother and I prepare food, care for the children, whether he actually likes my father more than he likes me…perhaps married me because of who my father was. Dangerous seeds to sow.

But he did gradually stop talking about his work to me; he slowly excluded me from its sphere. That is partly why I feel so alienated from him now: that knowledge is as clear as light breaking through a cloud and into a clear pool of water.

Partly…but there is another reason too. A reason I approach with reluctance, but with clarity, nevertheless. He disapproves of me, because he is entirely conservative at heart, and I have a fascination with the unconventional. He might make unusual furniture, but it is functional and solid and crafted, rather than highly imaginative; he might wring metals into delicate shapes and designs on commission, but he wants none of the objects in his house. He might know artists and craftspeople, but he has no desire to mix with them, my father excepted.

I remember a time we stayed at the camping ground on Stradbroke Island, at Cylinder Beach. The children were little, and we had borrowed a friend's four-man tent. In the shower block, I fell into conversation with another mother, and we had a drink with her that night. The next evening, she invited us to visit a friend of hers who lived at Main Beach, in a narrow three-storey unit with a staircase spiralling through its centre. We wound up to the top floor: to a large room divided into a living area and a bedroom by a bookcase, and with sliding glass doors to the southeast, taking in the dusk-dark inky scape of the Pacific, and, to the west, undulating forest edged with a sculpted scallop of sea.

The children had been fed and were playing happily with my new friend's two girls, so when joints were circulated, I accepted. I sensed immediately Mark's tension as I took the cigarette. But his disapproval faded as the drug entered my veins. I stared around the room, the voices of the others there fading out as Mark's reaction had. I looked at a twisted hatstand, realising after a moment that it was actually a branch of mangrove cut to stand in a pot of sand. On top of a beer fridge was a mannequin's bald head, swathed in iridescent scarves. There were bowls of feathers and flower petals, and mobiles of driftwood and shells suspended from the ceiling, and sarong-draped cushions on the mattress on which we reclined; there was a pinboard littered with photographs on one wall and a tapestry of three naked muses on another. Ropey blue and red and white candles lit the room, and their scent mingled with the pungent cannabis smoke and the blue cigarette smoke and the sickly smell of incense and the crooning tones of Van Morrison… And I loved it all. I felt comfortable, at home…but Mark did not. We left soon after. We had a huge row over it.

Why is that relevant? I ponder it as I wave to Charlotte as she calls to me and swoops down a slide. Because it is a suppression of my spirit, of my choices in life…it's paternalistic. Protective? Maybe. Well meaning? Probably. I sigh.

And I have still solved none of the problems Yanni has raised.

All right. Possibility number two. I brace myself. Yanni regrets the kiss, regrets the rekindling of the past…wants simply to clear the air for friendship between us… And I find myself shaking my head, physically, probably looking, if there was any other adult in the park to observe me, like some mad woman mumbling to herself. No. No. When Ross was two and I heard a rumour that Yanni had married, I used to daydream that he and I could become friends, that he and his wife and Mark and I could visit each other for dinner, or have lunchtime barbecues or bayside picnics – but even then I knew it would be too dangerous. Dangerous to our marriages. Dangerous because children were involved. Or dangerous to my own tenacious fantasies.

If that is what he wants, I will have nothing more to do with him…

I take a deep breath. Okay then. Possibility number three. Yanni has come back for me. Yanni loves me still, and wants me back. And I sit quite still. I close my eyes. It's too late, I think. It's too late. I'm married: I have children who need both Mark and me. I'm married, I feel owned. I'm married. I have made my choice.

What good could come of it? I think. What good can come of my meeting Yanni? How can I even contemplate meeting him? If he should say, I've come back for you…where could that lead? Only to disaster. Only to disaster.

And so I sit in the cold winter light watching my daughter laugh in the wind, and I wrestle with the image of the boy who has become a man and who has chosen so arrogantly to re-enter my life, and the image of my stern and protective husband who has not kissed me in more than a week, and I know what my choice has to be; I know that I will meet Yanni tomorrow, and I know what I have to say to him, and what I have to do…and my heart beats and beats, with the pounding of a funeral drum.

10

On the way back from the park, I run into my neighbour, Julia. She's pushing her twins Chantelle and Andrew in their double stroller. Julia's striding energetically, trying to burn off weight; she's been on an exercise program since the twins were born but her penchant for beesting pastries often counteracts its benefits.

'Venny! How was Stradbroke?'

'Great,' I say, 'really good.' She and her husband Brian always go to her parents' house for a late Sunday lunch and to church afterwards, so she doesn't know about Mark's cut and I don't really feel like going into it on the street.

'I can't stop. Have to keep my heart-rate up. Come over for a coffee later?'

'Okay.' I look after her with a warm heart: her baggy bottom wags at me as she thrusts the stroller up a rise. She's everything I'm not: gregarious and innocent, home-loving and contented. I could, and often do, listen to her for hours. She's like the friend I always wanted at school but never found because my family shifted so often I lost all my confidence in being able to make friends. It was only when I went to art college that the ability came back again.

Julia brings me back to earth. Charlotte is asleep in the stroller by the time I get home and I carry her carefully up the stone-cut steps, wrestle my key from a pocket, then put her gently in the spare bedroom we've constructed under the house. Her flushed cheeks and mouth, and lashes as curly as commas, make my heart soft as music. I kiss her as I tuck her in, and her cheek is soft and plump against my lips...

And the sudden spark of what I have decided to do tomorrow sets me in a panic. In that adrenalin rush, I leave the bed abruptly; I remember the washing isn't out and the floors aren't mopped and there are rooms to be tidied and other washing to be brought in from the line and folded – and I think, this isn't happening! This isn't happening! I have sudden flashes of Yanni's body, the tautness of the muscle between his hip and thigh, the golden halo of his hair – and I am fizzy with panic. I race around, starting one thing and remembering something else I have to do. I think, I can't do it. I can't do it. I can't wipe him out, cut him out of my dreams, cut him out of a possible future… but there is no possible future. So what should I do, what should I do?

Only one thing. Simply do all the other things I have planned for tomorrow and stand Yanni up.

I take a deep breath and stand upright, quite still. Yes.

The spare bedroom window is directly opposite and slightly below Julia's dining room since Julia lives right beside us on the lower side of the hill, so I leave Charlotte sleeping and go over to Julia's in my T-shirt sleeves. Despite my resolution, I'm still hot and nervous. And Julia is calm and cheerful, bubbling coffee in her Mr Cappuccino and cutting through the plum-purple skin of an avocado. Her twins are crawling and squealing through a maze of giant, primary-coloured foam blocks that she has set up for them in the lounge room.

We settle with our coffee and avocado and hot, crunchy bread and a plate of sticky cakes at the dining table, in a slant of winter sunlight. The twins immediately lose interest in the blocks and begin to climb on their mother, and from her to the white piano against the wall behind her. The piano keys plink and boom and Julia talks to me and ignores both the noise and the little bodies sinking their feet into her soft flesh.

After she's been through the antics of the twins in church and the idiosyncrasies of her family, she takes an abrupt mouthful of cake and says, 'I heard you guys fighting again before you went to Straddie. Same old thing?'

I sigh and shrug. 'Yup. He won't do things with us because he "has" to work, but he doesn't want me to do things without him. He certainly didn't want me to go to stay with Peri. Thinks she's a bad influence. That I'll drink too much with her, or smoke joints. Thinks she'll set me up with some bloke, too, probably. To spite him.' I smile, thinking then of Mick, the surfie, and Peri's reckless suggestion. 'The trouble is, he's probably right!'

And I immediately regret saying that. But when I look up, guiltily, at Julia, her eyes are large and calm and bright with interest…and I have a sudden desire to confide in her. I pause, sip my coffee, then decide to take the risk. 'Can I ask you something, Julia?'

'Fire away.'

'Would you ever have an affair?'

She stops chewing and looks suddenly wary. 'Me? Why?'

'Oh, I don't know. Just hypothetical, of course.'

We both look at the twins, one of whom has squealed.

I continue, with caution, 'But sometimes I do wonder whether it's natural to be monogamous. I mean, is it normal to only want sex with one person?' I stir my coffee deliberately, and glance up at her face for her reaction. 'Maybe Mark's right to be jealous… Maybe I would have an affair if it was offered and I had the opportunity and I was attracted enough. What do you think?'

Julia is frowning, but she nods, slowly, still looking at the twins. 'Maybe…'

'But –' I lean forward then, holding my coffee cup in front of me with both hands, forcing her to look at me, 'I wouldn't do it if it was only to satisfy some man's ego, or lust. I'd want it so I could touch someone else…his soul… But what do you think? Do you think there are thousands of women and men out there who secretly lust after some person they know, and only stay faithful to their partners because they're frightened of wrecking their marriages? Because it's better for children to have both parents living with them? Or because they're nice and secure, comfortable…or maybe just unimaginative?'

Julia is silent. Then she picks up her cup, sips and says, 'Oh, I don't know. For a lot of people, it's not really an option. And even if it was,

I think they'd dismiss it for all kinds of reasons – because they have all that history, you know, all that shared past with one other person, and that's more important than lust – and fear, fear of a new relationship not lasting, of being lonely...'

I stop listening, listening instead to my own troubled heart; then vaguely through that and the strident keys of the piano I hear her say, 'I almost had an affair. Last year.'

I jerk my head up, staring.

She nods. 'When the twins were tiny. I didn't – I didn't even meet the man – we just used to ring each other – we're old friends and he was having problems in his marriage and the twins were driving me crazy and Brian was hardly speaking to me let alone doing anything else. It's the Madonna/whore thing with him – when I'm pregnant or breastfeeding, he can't touch me. Then it came to a point where I – we, this man and I – had to make a decision. And I just thought, no. There was too much to lose – Brian would throw me out and fight to the death to keep Chantelle and Andrew and Monique if he ever found out – he just adores his kids. I'd lose everything – the kids, the house, Brian. It wasn't worth it. Plus, it's a huge sin.'

I watch her lips close on the last word righteously, as if that's the main argument. But of course it's not.

'How brave of you.' My voice is faint.

'Brave? Uh, uh. Wise, maybe. It was hard, I won't deny that – we had to agree never – never – to speak to each other again. Have any contact. It was too much of a temptation.'

And I go cold. I can feel the blood turning to iced water my brain. Never to have contact again... Never to speak... I shake my head slightly, staring at her, and get my tongue to move. 'But did it have to be that way? Couldn't you have been really careful? Or still remained friends? I mean, you said you were old friends. Does admitting sexual attraction destroy that?' I bite my lip, agitated.

Julia purses her mouth, and helps Andrew on his climb over her thighs. Then she looks back at me and her gaze is steady. 'It was too strong.' Her voice is matter-of-fact. 'It would have shown. I would have been too happy, for one thing. I already was, a bit... And someone would have got hurt. One of us three. Maybe all. That's why God made the commandment: to protect us all.' The twins are marching on the piano again, and she raises her voice as she says that last, to be heard over the bass notes.

And then the doorbell suddenly rings. I get up restlessly while Julia's away, the twins scampering after her, and look in on Charlotte – you can see straight into our downstairs room from Julia's when the curtains are open. Charlotte hasn't moved.

Julia comes back carrying a big bunch of flowers. 'They're for my birthday.' She's grinning hugely. 'From Brian. The rat – it gets him out of having to buy me a real present. Doesn't matter – I've bought my present for myself anyway.'

'Oh – I didn't know – happy birthday!' I hug her and she keeps smiling, her cheeks pink. 'What are you doing for it?'

'Oh, nothing...'

'Well, come over for dinner.' I think quickly, and dismiss Mark's mood. Bugger him, I think. 'Really! I'm making chicken cacciatore and spaghetti – we always have heaps – it's nothing special but it's better than cooking for yourself – come over, please!'

She looks at me with her head on one side. 'Well, thanks. All right. That'd be nice.' She still looks embarrassed.

'I'd better go. I have to get the groceries before I pick up Ross. And the twins look like they're ready for their nap.' They've both started to whinge, each tugging at one of Julia's baggy jeans' legs.

'No way. If we're coming over to your place, I won't let them sleep now. Then they'll be in bed by six. I can keep them awake all right till then, can't I, guys?' She begins to tickle them both and their whinges turn to squeals of delight.

When Mark comes home, I tell him I've invited Julia over, and for a moment I think he's going to snap at me. Then instead, he swings into one of the moods that first attracted me to him – an energetic and frisky mood, full of panache. He turns to the children. 'Julia's birthday! Well, that's a special occasion. What shall we do for her, Ross? Charlotte? I've got an idea. Come on, let's go up to the shed.'

I stare after his limping form and the dancing children uncertainly.

While I cook, they're busy in the shed. Then I hear them hammering on the back deck. When I go out, Mark is hooking up candle lanterns made from intricate twists of gold I know he's been making on commission from just about Brisbane royalty. In the corner of the deck stands a tall candlestick made from polished, wind-braided mangrove branches. That's what they've made in the shed. It's exquisite…something he would never want to have in our house. He doesn't look at me but his face is triumphant.

I take the children in to bath them and Mark goes out in the car. He comes back with bottles of Chianti and fresh calamari and Italian bread and ice cream cake. He prepares the calamari and makes up a chilli sauce to cook it in.

When Julia comes over, she's so embarrassed by the fuss she blushes. Brian is sheepish. We drink a lot and eat everything, and Mark out-talks Julia and ignores me completely and has everyone except me entertained and happy. Ross and Sharlie and Monique race around excitedly till ten o'clock, when I finally get them to settle. When they're asleep, I wash the dishes in the semi-dark kitchen so Julia won't come and help. I swipe the dishes and look out through the kitchen window at Mark's burly, bearded profile and the companionable couple opposite him, and at the new candlestick, its light flickering like a lonely heart in the quiet darkness.

11

I don't sleep well. When the phone rings at seven the next morning, I'm up and as jumpy as a fever pulse. I snatch the receiver. 'Yes?'

'Venny? It's Aunt Dem.' The voice is clipped and matter-of-fact, slightly guttural, but fresh – as if she's been up for hours. 'I'm in Brisbane.'

'Aunt Dem!' My voice squeaks.

'You've been to see Peri, I gather.'

I put my hand on my chest and take two deep breaths. 'I... Well, yes, we got back on Sunday – Mark's cut his leg –'

'Good. Meet me for lunch today? The Shingle Inn. Midday. What's that you say?'

'Mark's cut himself with the circular saw...'

'Hospital?'

'No, no – he's home...twelve stitches.'

'Walking?'

'Yes – with a limp.'

'Oh, well, that's all right. Done worse to m'self. Give him some aspirin, keep him in bed. Can do without you for a couple of hours, can't he?'

'Well, yes...'

'Midday all right with you, then?'

'No!' I shake my head, my brain stupid, frozen. 'No! No! S–sorry Aunt Dem – I have to work, I... How about tomorrow instead?' My voice is breathless as I finish.

'Tomorrow?'

'I'll have to bring Charlotte, of course...but I work today, remember? At the art shop...'

'Art shop? Had forgotten. Hmm, well, if today's out of the question… Righto. Twelve. See you then.'

'Okay…' The phone beeps in my ear. I stare at it for a moment, then put it slowly back in its cradle.

I am early at Kodak Beach. I stand in the winter sun, looking at the artificial shore and its too-clean, too-calm lagoon. Papery leaves blow along the path between me and the sand. Near the water, two little boys are playing with plastic supermarket bags in the still blustery wind. The smaller boy throws his bag erratically then plunges after it, mimicking the older one, who flies his like a parachute, throwing it into the air then tossing up his arms and chin to catch it. I have a moment of blind panic. I look around in confusion, grab at my bag, wrestle for my keys –

Then Yanni is there, beside me, smiling down.

I step back, staring at him. His irises are the thing – they're like a scent I connect indelibly with an exact time and place – their colour is like no other I've ever seen on a human being. But it's more than that, it's more than their colour. It's their wide-apartness, and a sort of catlike laziness, and the way they look at you, hold you in their smile, as if you're the only one, the only thing, that matters. He has a silver earring, and a leather thong around his neck, and a jumper slung around his shoulders. He's wearing jeans and a white T-shirt advertising a U2 concert, and the white shirt makes his eyes even more intense.

He's still smiling. He hasn't shaved, and the bristles on his face make him look like a teenager still: just a shadow of soft growth, not enough for a beard. He has dimples and full lips. It's the colours of his face that make him unusual: the unflawed brown and pink skin, the startling aquamarine of his eyes with their unsettling gaze, the gold points of stubble on his face and the straight bleached fall of hair to his collar. He could be a bushranger or a pirate, someone who steals your heart along with your purse.

I can't move. I stare up at him.

He hesitates, and the smile is less certain; I think he is waiting for me to touch him, to kiss him perhaps, but I can't move. Then he abruptly loops his arm through mine and steers me to the right and we're walking, and I can feel the body warmth of his skin and the prickly brush of the hairs on his forearm against mine. I take a breath and turn to him and I'm suddenly smiling back and I'm okay.

'Sorry about that phone call.' He ducks his head obliquely with a half-grin – a gesture I'd forgotten. 'Dutch courage, or something.'

I move my shoulders and an eyebrow slightly. 'That's okay.' I look at him sideways. 'Where are we going?'

'Just – I don't know. To the real water, maybe? The river? Too many kids around here.'

It's true: there are children paddling in the lagoons; children in prams and strollers being pushed by us; groups of mothers at picnic tables and barbecue areas and playgrounds. The sun is beautifully warm as long as you're not in the wind: it seems to have brought the playgroups out. I dismiss the pang of pain his reaction to the children elicits in me, and avert my gaze from toddlers paddling in the artificial streams and rock pools as we head down to the river boardwalk.

From the unprotected river, the wind is blustery again. I shiver, and untie my jacket from my waist to pull it on. Then I have broken contact with Yanni; and I hesitate, longing to make it again, but knowing I shouldn't, I mustn't.

He brushes a hand over his chin, and adjusts the jumper on his shoulders, then gestures to a bench facing the river. 'How about here?'

We sit without touching each other. My back is rigid, and I hunch my shoulders a little inside the jacket. I look out at the wrinkled river and swallow. My heart begins to pound. But beside me Yanni lounges, his arms along the back of the bench, an ankle cocked on the opposite knee.

'So,' he says, 'Venny.'

'Yes.' And suddenly I'm struck by the wonder of it. Here is Yanni, after all these years, sitting beside me, alone, saying my name. And here am I, so close all I need to do is move my hand…

I gasp, and clasp my hands together, and stand up abruptly. 'I… It's so cold! I – do you want a drink? I think I want a drink –'

'Sure.' He's raised his eyebrows in surprise: then he smiles, all the beauty in the world flooding from those aquamarine seas into my face. 'What does Venny the wife drink these days? Chardonnay, perhaps? I'm sure it wouldn't be…Summer Wine any more! Or Green Ginger…do you remember the taste of that stuff? The way it burned…'

And he's looking right into my eyes and into my soul, and I see his memory as clearly as if he has transmitted it into my head via satellite: at me passing the bottle from my lips to his, and lowering my mouth around his penis, and his eyelids slanted at me, then closing…

'Groucho like Green Ginger Wine?' he asks slowly, still staring at the memory.

'Groucho?'

'What Peri calls your husband.'

I freeze. But whether it's more at the insult to Mark or the suggested intimacy between Yanni and Peri I'm not sure. 'I… His name's Mark,' I say, shaking my head. 'And – Peri doesn't know him that well.' I turn away from him, back toward the restaurants and bars. 'Come on.'

We find a table behind plate glass in a restaurant looking over a walkway. The glass is good: its view gives me something to look at besides Yanni.

Yanni orders easily, with just the right amount of confidence. It's this which makes him older, I think absently: except for a few fine lines around his eyes he could be anywhere between twenty and thirty; it's his sureness and polish which reveal his age.

We drink Chardonnay. I have suggested it – a good one – to get back at him. He arches his eyebrows and I think he's going to have a beer instead – then doesn't. He watches me all the time the waitress fusses, so that I feel unnerved again. When she's gone, we sip wine in unison, and, flushing, I turn to the walkway view. Then I think, this is ridiculous. I've got to take control.

'So,' I say, taking a breath, leaning back casually and looking directly at him, 'tell me about what's happened since I last saw you. 'Course, I read in the paper years ago that you'd made the trials to Hawaii –'

I stop because his eyes are dazzling – and I pick up my glass hurriedly. 'Well, I know you lost the heats in Bondi one year, but you got in the next and it was big news up here. The underdog thing, you know. And then when you made Hawaii...'

'You followed all that?' He's broken me off.

I nod silently, feeling my heart flutter onto my sleeve. 'Didn't you think I would?' I almost whisper it.

He's quiet for a moment, staring at me. Then he says abruptly, 'I got accepted into uni as well, you know. Sydney Uni, Human Movement. Thought I might be a phys. ed. teacher. That's what Mum wanted me to be. Solid career, solid income, respectable. But I couldn't get into it. The thought of spending my life in schools, indoors...' He fiddles with the stem of his glass, frowning slightly, then sips the wine and looks back at me.

When I don't say anything, he goes on, 'So I dropped out and got a job in a Bondi surf shop. And then Mum married a rich Greek businessman – she and Dad got divorced, did you know?'

I shake my head.

He goes on, 'Well, you know what she's like when it comes to Greece and Greeks. Maybe because Dad wasn't quite the real thing ... no, that wasn't really it – he...' He stops, looking at me, then shrugs. 'Anyway, they set me up in my own shop on the island. Sounds like I sponged off them, but I designed a new surfboard and made a bit from that and then Mum got in on the act and got a label happening on a line of surf gear. Even though I didn't make it in Hawaii. Then I did a bit of travelling up north, surfing, selling the label. Anywhere there were waves.'

The waitress comes back with a bowl of nuts. 'Complimentary,' she says, trying to catch his eye.

But Yanni's gaze blazes at me across the table as he says, 'Thanks,' and until she's gone; then abruptly he looks at the bowl and offers it to me. 'And now I'm back. What about you?'

I shake my head at the nuts. 'Me? Well, I – after you left, I was a bit restless. I dropped out of my course and found a job. Decided to save and go to Europe, see the world, you know. What most people do. Then when I came back I went back to college, and I met Mark. And then I was pregnant – you said Luke told you...' I break off because he's grunted. I raise an eyebrow at him.

He shrugs and takes a handful of nuts. 'Knew it wasn't for love.'

And I'm stung by his arrogance. 'Oh, yeah?' I hold my wine glass in mid-air and narrow my eyes at him.

He tilts his head to the side. 'Well, was it?'

I stare at him – and I don't know how to answer. He sits waiting, still, watching me; and slowly all my defensiveness drains away.

I chew my bottom lip, and put the glass down. Then I say deliberately and quietly, 'If there was love then, there's not a lot left now.'

And we're both silent.

Then after a moment he says, 'I've got this job offer, from Sydney again – to manage a surf shop down there. I have to let them know pretty soon... I just wanted to...'

And then he ducks his head sideways again, and the dimple shows, and I have no idea what he really means. But my heart begins to pound.

But before I have a chance to say anything, Yanni sits up and leans toward me, picks up his glass and swigs the wine and takes another fistful of nuts, and says briskly, 'So, tell me about Europe. Where did you go – Greece, at all?'

And so I start to tell him a story about my trip to Greece, and then he interrupts with a similar experience in north Queensland of all places – we get back on track and he interrupts again; I interrupt him – we begin to laugh and he holds my gaze while I talk and I watch his face unashamedly as his stories unfold. We finish the wine and the nuts and we talk and talk, as if we have both been uncorked and all the impressions of our lives have to pour out, all the past decade has to be written out in scrawled outline, hurriedly, sketchily, in case the ink should run out before we can finish. And one o'clock looms and I find a telephone and ring the art shop and assume an artificial voice and say that Venny's sick and can't make it today; and then I've sliced off my real life neatly, pretending it doesn't exist, not even acknowledging that I have anything to do with it.

12

When I wake, rain is falling softly on the window, like tears. The room is filled with a green light, as if our lovemaking has generated it; it is in fact caused by a shaft of dusk sun shining through the rain and a heavy gown of tree fern. Sometime between one o'clock and now, the wind must have changed and rain set in.

Yanni sleeps facing me. He looks like a baby sleeping. His eyelashes curl like fronds and his skin is smooth and plump and childish. He sleeps with his left arm under my neck. I watch dreams flicker across his eyelids and remember another time I have done this, in another life and another world.

I rise and wrap his shirt around my body. I look back at him and the light has faded and the warmth is draining from the room, and he sleeps on, his left arm still cradling the space where I have been.

I wash in the bathroom. The sink is olive porcelain and underneath the tap is an ugly brown stain, like an old bloodstain. I wash my face and dry it on a scratchy striped towel and fix my make-up. Then I dress in my jeans and shirt.

In the lounge room, there's a man rolling a joint and watching television. He must be back from work because he has on neat, pressed blue clothes; he looks odd, rolling a fat joint with a harmonica dangling beside his tie.

'Hi,' I say.

'G'day. Have a nice afternoon?'

'Yes.'

'Want some of this?'

'No, thanks. I have to go. Yanni staying with you?'

'For a couple of days.' He lights the cigarette and blows out a long stream of smoke. 'Usually stays here when he's over from the island.' He holds up the cigarette. 'Don't mind, long as he keeps bringing me the good stuff.'

'Does he – does he often have –'

He's looking at me quizzically, his head back and eyelids half-closed. 'What?'

There are so many things I want to know that we haven't even brushed on. About him, about his life, about how he has turned out. Things I need to ask him, though.

'It's nothing. Goodbye,' I say. 'Tell Yanni I had to go, will you? But I'll be home Friday, if he wants to contact me.'

'Sure.' He drags again on the cigarette and the scent of it and the poignant notes of the harmonica drift after me as I walk out into the falling night.

It is only when I am driving home and the rain has cleared that I have a sudden, overwhelming vision of myself as others might see me. Stopping at a traffic light, I stare out at a row of Americana – McDonald's and Hungry Jack's and Red Rooster – plastic, fantasy-catering food stops as stereotyped and shallow as bride dolls, as Barbie's Motor Home-life, as Action Man – and I think, oh my God, I've become just like that. I've become a plastic, make-believe loving wife and mother – a shadow wife with no heart. Here I am, driving in my shiny silver Laser down a street lined with America, going home to my trendy timber home with views of the city and double garage, to my two children, a boy and a girl, and my hard-working but inattentive husband – and underneath the polished exterior I have as much virtue as the Medusa...

Only it isn't like that. It isn't that I lack morality, integrity – it's much more complicated than that – it's all tied up with anxiety and sexuality and deep, deep loneliness, and three-o'clock in the morning insecurities seeping into the reality of dawn... It's all tied up with frustration and boredom and loneliness and loneliness... It's all tied up for me with a quest for happiness and my unhappiness and my life taking on the shape and taste and tightness of the loneliness of the past.

I park outside the house. I am anxious, my hands shaking a little and my breathing shallow. I feel guilty and therefore frightened, unreasonably: an old fear connected with childhood fear of my father, of male authority. I climb the rocky steps to the yard and the flight of stairs to the front veranda. Through the opaque glass of the French doors, I can see blue television light fluttering. The front door is locked and I turn my key briskly and stride in.

'Mummy!' Charlotte rolls onto her belly and tumbles to her feet, and runs to me with her arms open.

I catch her up and bury my face in her silky fall of hair.

'Where have you been, Mum?' Ross has turned in his chair but makes no move to me.

'Come and give me a hug.' He comes willingly, sheepishly, half-smiling, and I bend and hold him. 'I got stuck in traffic, darling.' The lie slips slickly off my tongue as if I have rehearsed it, as I most certainly must have in some secret, unrecognised part of my brain. I lie easily, but not without guilt. 'How was school?'

'Good.' He's already lost interest in me: his eyes are back on the television. I drop Charlotte on the couch and he sinks back beside her, his eyes still glued to the screen.

Mark is in the kitchen. 'You're late.' The words are a statement but his eyebrows touch his hair. He's looking at me at least; that's always the first step to our reconciliation when he's unwinding from anger with me.

I sigh with relief and the tight knot of fear in my belly loosens. 'Yes. An accident: traffic was banked up for miles. I should have caught the train in, but I was running a bit late. How's the leg?' I notice the limp as he moves between the stove and the sink.

'All right. Your mother rang.'

'Oh?'

'Mmm. Worried about Peri. Your aunt's been talking to her. Thinks she's getting into all sorts of mischief on the island – drugs the latest thing.'

I feel a stab of guilt. I've been so wrapped up in myself I've hardly thought of Peri, and of what I'll say to Aunt Dem tomorrow. 'Well, I didn't see any sign of it.' Except maybe the jitteriness – and thinness. But those could have been from tens of different things. 'I'll give her a ring later.'

He doesn't say anything more, so I open the fridge and pick at a platter of cut-up cheese and apples, leftovers from the children's afternoon snack. 'You collect the kids all right?' Mark finishes early on Tuesdays to free me up a little and have time with Ross and Charlotte; it's his one concession to his working life for the children.

'Mmm.'

'Drink?' I say.

'What have we got?'

'Cask white.' I pour two glasses. 'What're you cooking?'

'Spag bol.'

'Smells good. I'm starving.'

He grunts and turns back to the pan.

I carry the cheese and my wine in to the children. I sit between them on our dusty, cosy Genoa and Charlotte immediately crawls onto my lap and snuggles, sucking her thumb. '*Twins of Destiny*?' I say.

Ross doesn't answer. Television absorbs him.

'Can I have a drink, Mummy?'

'Milk?'

'Chocolate milk.'

'Dinner's nearly ready. Plain milk now.' I lift her off my legs and find and fill her special cup. I sit down again with her on my lap and look at the program but I don't watch it.

The wine lifts me and floats me back to Yanni. He becomes like a subliminal message, flashes of touch and sound and vision flicking in and out of my consciousness. As he has been once before.

And it is strange, but as I sit there, Charlotte on my lap, I realise I don't feel guilty about this secret consciousness. I feel guilty about deceiving Mark; I feel guilty about lying to the children; but I don't feel guilty about thinking about, remembering, Yanni. And it occurs to me that this is because I am always slipping in and out of secret worlds anyway – the private sanctuaries in my mind of art and books and memories of holidays and plans for my children, for example – these worlds are always there, relieving the boredom or stress of living in the present. I remember doing this all through my childhood too: dreaming then of dancing or a boy, of achievement or romance. You get used to relying on things like that, I guess.

I think, but you've committed a crime. Only it's not a crime, not technically: adultery is not against the law. Then I think, this has nothing to do with the present, nothing to do with Mark and the children; it's more as if time has become mixed, and Yanni's and my lovemaking happened outside the present – as if I passed like Lucy in *The Lion, the Witch and the Wardrobe* into a fantasy world, out of which I passed just as easily, with no real time passed at all. And somewhere inside me I know that this is not true, but that I have to keep believing it. I have to believe that Yanni is make-believe, an escape from the real world – and I suddenly understand the attraction of America, of McDonald's and Hungry Jack's and Barbie's Motor Home… That maybe all of us need some fantasy into which we feel we can escape. The trick is to continue to recognise the reality of one and the transience of the other.

And for me that has to be easy. Because Yanni really does come from another time. The thing between Yanni and me began in the distant past, in the hazy memory of childhood, in the innocent days when touching each other's bodies was wholly a pleasure, untainted by guilt or subterfuge, and the certainty of seeing his face every morning was what held my life together, what sustained me, animated me – what literally gave me life. Being with Yanni is all tied up with things from another time: romantic love and loyalty and faith in something spiritual, something which wouldn't exist if either Yanni or I denied that it did, but to which I cling as perhaps my last transcendent experience in a string of such experiences, the rest of which have faded to nothing, illusions, every one.

13

I park on Albert Street, on the hill up to Wickham Terrace. I take the stroller from the boot and lift Charlotte, who has fallen asleep in the warmth of the car, into it: but despite my gentleness, she wakes. I sigh: her afternoon sleep routine is totally disrupted now. She has only had a ten-minute nap, and she'll eat the wrong things at the café, which Aunt Dem will buy for her, and then be overtired by six, sleep too early and wake tomorrow at dawn… But of course it's my own fault. I started the disruption of the routine by going to the island on the weekend. And I shouldn't have agreed to this time: I should have said, no, how about one-thirty? I could have fed Charlotte a healthy lunch and she would have slept through the transfer from car to stroller…

I have a lot to learn about saying no, still. Even though I've turned thirty.

I'm worried about what to say to Aunt Dem, too. About Peri. What should I reveal: that she's keen on Yanni, and that's why she's staying on the island? But that is a fool's paradise. He doesn't care for her.

Or that Haden visits her, and that she's not unaccommodating to his attention? But that there is a band of bruise around one of her wrists that wasn't there when I went out with her on Saturday…

Or that part of her defection to the island has to do with her rebellion against Aunt Dem.

Sure. All of that. Not. Aunt Dem has lived in the country all her life, and has a hearty suspicion of anything remotely unwholesome. She herself married a Proserpine Italian – Catholic, of course – after a highly respectable courtship, and worked hard with him on their farm for ten years before she conceived Peri – a child they thought they would never have. Then her husband was killed in a road accident when Peri was six. So she's understandably doubly protective of Peri: because Peri was such a precious gift, and because Aunt Dem has no one else.

I sigh again, steering Charlotte's stroller between gaps in the pavement, breathing in the Queensland Rail fumes from Roma Street below, wishing that one day they'd do something about the eyesore the rail-yards infect, and that I had some solutions myself to my own nagging problems.

The Shingle Inn is as enticing as it was when I was a teenager, going there with Mum and Aunt Dem and Peri when they were in town. Aunt Dem used to come to Brisbane irregularly, but probably most often at Exhibition time, when her other farmer mates were down. I don't know what sugar cane had to do with the farmer mates and beef and horses but I'd refused to learn, anyway. My mother used to berate me about my lack of interest in the outside world but I always had the excuse to fall back on. I was like my father. An artist. And she never criticised him, so I, by extension, became excused as well. To the point I suppose of her despair…and who could blame her?

But the Shingle Inn was, and is, the representation of Class to me, and to Aunt Dem. It has two bowed display windows, on either side of the entrance. These are multi-paned, with the divisions in timber. Beneath the glass are cakes made in the image of every child's fantasy. Everything glitters with sugar, shines with sugar glaze, is etched in chocolate, or pouts custard or rippled cream. Inside, you drink whipped iced coffee, cinnamon-powdered chocolate malts, or frothy sweet cappuccino. Everywhere there's mirror-shiny glass and chrome and timber and warm wood. Nothing plastic in sight.

The problem, though, is it's not made for children. Or more particularly, strollers. There are two narrow steps before a narrow push-in door. Very wise, of course, really.

I'm saved by a tall thin man in a green coat. He holds the door open, slips me a sideways smile, helps me with the wheels. And there is Aunt Dem, sitting at a window table, her grey-streaked head already bent over a silver pot of tea and a menu.

'Hi, Aunt Dem.'

'Venny.' She slips her glasses from her nose, so they dangle from a chain around her neck, and lifts her still-black eyebrows at me; and in their familiar dark hollows her brown eyes flash a smile.

I bend to kiss her cheek, noticing its cool dryness, and her scent of soap and lipstick. Lipstick is one of her signs of dressing up for town; another is the neat chignon into which she has pulled her hair. I've plaited my own hair down my back in deference to her image of me, which I have no intention of spoiling.

'Charlotte.' She pats Charlotte's chin with a short-nailed, vein-ropey hand.

There's no room for the stroller at the table. I lift Charlotte from it and onto one of the two spare chairs, and fold the carriage swiftly. There's a space against the wall where I can prop it. Charlotte stares solemnly from Aunt Dem to me.

I sit down breathlessly. 'Sorry I'm a bit late – have you been here long?'

'Oh, no. But service isn't what it used to be. Have to order at the counter, bring the tray over yourself. Quick enough, though, I suppose.' She says the last grudgingly, lifting a shoulder under its countrywoman's jacket. 'Here – have my menu. Think I'll have toasted sandwiches. Always did a good job with those.

'Charlotte –' she leans toward my daughter and pats her dungareed knee, 'You have a look in the window here. Come on, I won't bite. Have a look, choose what you like.'

Charlotte slips a little reluctantly from her chair, but I can see the window is too enticing to resist. She stands beside my aunt and presses her nose against the glass.

I settle on toasted sandwiches and tea as well, and Charlotte, with a sideways look at me that just manages to avoid my eyes, points to a large profiterole covered in shiny chocolate sauce. I order for all of us, taking the twenty-dollar bill Aunt Dem places under the sugar bowl, knowing it is useless to argue with her. Surprisingly, while I'm at the counter, Charlotte stays at the table, nodding or shaking her head to

Aunt Dem's questions. She's beginning to know which side her bread is buttered on, I think wryly.

With food in front of us, I relax a little. I tell Aunt Dem about Mark's accident, and ask about the farm and Proserpine in general. And then suddenly we're on to Peri.

'Look,' Aunt Dem begins abruptly, wiping her fingers on a serviette, 'I don't care if she wants to stay on that island for a bit. Not really. What I don't want is her dumping her degree when she's only got one year to go. What I don't want is her getting mixed up in drugs. She might be twenty-eight, but that doesn't mean she's got any sense.' Her lips clamp down firmly on the last word.

I push back a strand of hair which has slipped from its plait, and pick up my teacup. 'I – don't think she'll get addicted to drugs, Aunt Dem! Mum said you were worried about that. Where on earth did you get the idea from?'

'I know what young people are like on that island. Hippies! Layabouts and bludgers. Should never have let her go on holiday with you when she was a teenager – that's where all this arty stuff started.'

'I used to go there all the time, Aunt Dem,' I say defensively, 'and I never came across hard drugs. Besides – she's good at art. She won all those prizes at school…'

'So did you! But you're not living on an island in some hippie commune, are you? Art's a hobby. Not a way of life.' She's looking cross, her brown eyes flashing.

'She's not in a commune – she's by herself, in a beautiful house. And Dad managed to make a living as an artist…'

'Yes, at what cost to you lot? Dragging you from town to town. Your poor mother never able to put down roots. Get herself a job.' The vertical lines near her mouth are tense.

'Mum never minded…'

'Course she did!' The phrase is snapped.

Wow, I think, did she? Did she really? And I never knew – I never realised.

'Your father was always in control. She just put up with it. Though she nearly left him, once.'

She puts her chin up as she says the last, and I stare at her in surprise. The expression in her eyes has changed…there's something challenging there now. I feel confused. Is there something she's trying to tell me? I frown, then shake my head. Surely she's exaggerating. My parents have had their fights, like any couple, but Mum has never contemplated leaving Dad. Surely.

'She told me, no one else.' She crumples her serviette decisively, still watching me.

I know my mother so little, I think. As little as she really knows me, perhaps? And yet…

I look automatically at Charlotte and notice she has finished the profiterole, and has begun to wriggle. I pull a colouring book and pens from my bag, shift her messy plate, wipe her face and set her things up.

I straighten my back. 'Well…even if she did, that's beside the point. It's Peri we're talking about.'

'Yes.' Aunt Dem pauses, then drops her gaze and pours more tea into her cup. Her voice becomes brisk again. 'And she's vulnerable.' She sips, then seems to make up her mind about something. She puts her chin up again, and her cup with a clatter down, and says, 'She's just like her father.'

I frown at her, with my head on one side. 'I'm…not sure I know what you mean.'

'You know what happened to him?'

'He was killed in a car crash…'

'Drink driving. Slave to booze.' She folds her arms and her mouth purses and pulls back at the corners. 'Can see it in Peri. Same addictive personality. Unstable. That's why I want her out of there. Back home, where she'll have routine, hard work – away from temptation. Where I can look after her.' And then her mouth falls, and her eyes frown a little – as if she's thinking of mangled cars and broken bodies, and her daughter when she was just a little thing – and I glance at Charlotte, sitting sticky-faced and innocent and very good, 'colouring in', on her best be-haviour.

Still frowning, I look down at my teacup. 'Isn't it up to her? She is twenty-eight.'

'Nonsense. Doesn't matter how old she is. She lacks your strength of character. But she'll listen to you, more than me.' Her voice is brisk and clipped again.

Strength of character! Oh, if only she knew! I shake my head, gri-macing away the beginnings of an ironic smile. 'Doubt it.'

'Venny.' She forces my face up. 'At least go and talk to her again, will you? She respects you. She won't have a bar of me.' Her chin is lifted and the hollows around her eyes are prominent again, and she's pleading. Aunt Dem, pleading!

I bite my bottom lip, then nod. 'Okay.' As if my heart has not begun to pound with the idea of going to the island again, as if I am not trying to quell fear, excitement, hope. I take a deep breath. 'Sure. Don't know what good it'll do but I'll go…when I can.' I feel treachery flooding my veins, leaking from my thumping heart. Poor Aunt Dem! What train of events is she unwittingly starting?

I meet her eyes, and half smile.

14

Friday. I wake with a heart so light it could be weightless. Mark is curled against my back; sometime in the night I touched him, put my arms around him; and we made love in the dark, quickly, fiercely. Now he's holding me, all the anger drained away. And I am light with this relief, with this lifted cloud, as I always am when we make up…and light too with that other excitement which I refuse to confront, but which quickens my pulse, nevertheless.

I cook breakfast: bacon, cheese and tomato grilled, the children's favourite. I ignore Ross's teasing and separate Charlotte gently from him when she begins to react. She helps me make toast and Ross skulks off; when I glance into his bedroom I see he's found a half-finished Meccano crane and is busy with it.

Mark comes up behind me while I'm at the stove and he kisses my neck. He's come out of the shower and his beard is soft and damp and soapy-smelling, and his hand inside my wrap is warm and strong. 'I love you,' he whispers.

I nod mutely. I know he's waiting for me to say the same thing to him, and I'm about to…and then the words thicken on my tongue. I don't know what I feel, I realise, besides relief that the tension between us is over. I don't know what I feel for him…

'How's the leg?' I ask instead, looking over my shoulder.

He shrugs. 'Not great. Hurt my knee when I was a kid, and this is making it play up again. But – see what happens when it heals.'

I frown and nod.

Then Ross interrupts with, 'Come on, Mum, I'm hungry!' and I jump and catch the griller just in time to stop it burning the toast.

Later when Mark has left and Ross is at school and Charlotte's settled in front of *Play School*, I'm bursting with energy. I scrub the bath and sink, throw all the towels in the washing machine and strip the beds. The bedrooms are shadowy in the winter morning, but a shaft of light swims across Charlotte's bed like the after-effect of my morning mood on her. I twist my fingers in its warmth for a moment, as I might in water, trying to touch something in myself...

And then sink down slowly on the bed, in the patch of light. I know why I'm happy. I know where this energy comes from. I know why I cuddled Mark in the night, why I had to get rid of the tension in the house. Because Yanni might come today.

God, I think: what am I doing? I can't do this. I can't keep doing this. I can't betray Mark like this! I'm not going to leave him. I'm not going to break up my family. Am I?

I shiver suddenly, despite the warmth of the light patch.

What does Yanni want from me? I'm being a fool. He doesn't want me, and two kids, and half a mortgage. He doesn't love me. He didn't come back, and now it's too late. That's all. That's what I have to tell him, if he comes.

I close my eyes. I remember Aunt Dem's words, about Peri. She lacks your strength of character. Have that, I think. Have strength of character. Please.

It's while I'm pegging out the sheets that Yanni turns up. Even though I'm half-expecting him, his lithe form with its blond hair blinding in the sun shocks me. For a moment, I'm back on Stradbroke, waiting for him to meet me at our cave, watching him moving along the beach toward me, his board under his arm.

But 'Hi,' I manage to say. 'Thought you might drop in.' I gulp air against a sheet, steadying myself. I can't let him see how he affects me – how he's hounded my dreams, how I'd held him in my head even when I least expected it, saddled him with such a burden of hope – hopelessly.

'Did you now?'

'Mmm. Sorry about leaving without saying goodbye but I had to get back.'

He comes towards me and I duck between two sheets. He follows me in and takes my mouth in his. The sheets are cool and damp around us.

'No!' I say; then, lamely, 'Julia might see.'

His breath is hot in my ear and the adrenalin is pumping around my body.

He walks behind me up the back steps and into the kitchen. Once inside, I'm edgy, nervous; I turn my back on him and begin taking clean cups and plates from the draining rack and putting them away. He arrests me. He places his hands around my waist. I feel his penis like an insistent child against my back.

His kisses on my neck make me shiver, but I push him away. He holds my waist still, though, and turns me to him. Then he cups my face in his hands. 'I love you, Venny,' he whispers, so quietly that I can barely make out the words. 'I love you and you love me. I know you do.'

How long have I dreamed of him saying such things? I must be asleep, I think. I'm only dreaming. But his hands are warm and smooth and the scent of aftershave is herbal and strong, far too strong to be in a dream...

And then suddenly, vividly, I'm reminded of Mark: of Mark saying 'I love you' too and kissing me at the stove with his soapy smelling beard and his hand inside my wrap. And I stand quite still, and take a big, shuddering breath.

'Love?' I say. 'What's that? I don't know what that is. I thought – I once thought –' I stare at him. Then I say abruptly, 'I love my children – fiercely. That's love. Love that doesn't abandon. Leave. Forget. Come back when it wants something. With no explanations.'

His eyes are shining, filled with light, smiling and beautiful, as if he hasn't heard the challenge in my voice. 'I'll tell you,' he says. 'I'll tell you what happened.'

I stare at him; I don't smile back. I lift his hands from my face, and clasp them. 'Well?'

'Not here. Not now. It's... Can you get away? Come back to the house with me...'

'No. I have Charlotte.' But in spite of my determination, my heart has quickened.

'Can't you drop her at a neighbour's, or something?' His voice is light, teasing.

I grimace. 'No. She's not a pet. No. I'm sorry.' The adrenalin is making my edginess sharp.

'Ven, I have to get back to Sydney tomorrow...'

'And I have to take Ross to soccer, and Charlotte to get a haircut,' and his mouth is on mine, his lips moving softly, warm cushions that soften all of my strength, all of my character.

After a while, he moves back, and he looks at me again. Wordlessly.

I look down at his hands, which I still clasp. 'But it's hopeless,' I whisper, 'isn't it?' I look up again, and we stare at each other.

In the silence, the final notes of *Play School* rise.

I am brought back to earth. I push him away from me just in time as Charlotte's feet pad on the polished boards. He turns to her as she comes round the doorway.

She stops, staring at him. I glance at him too, and see, to my astonishment, that his expression is one of surprise.

Then his face relaxes. 'Hello,' he says, smiling. 'Well, aren't you like your mother?'

She doesn't reply; she creeps over to me and catches my skirt. I pick her up automatically.

'You'd better go,' I say. 'We have to go out – I've made arrangements –'

He stands still, irresolute, looking at us both.

'But –' and the words have tumbled out before I can check them – 'I saw Aunt Dem, Peri's mother, yesterday. She wants me to go back to the island, to talk to Peri again... It'll be in a couple of weeks...'

He nods, then semi-smiles. 'Okay. I'll be in Sydney a week. Give us a ring when I get back.' He digs in his pocket and pulls out a card. 'The number's on here.' He hesitates. 'I can pick you up from Dunwich, if you like.'

'Well...I'll see. Thanks for the offer.'

He hesitates again, still looking at us. 'Okay… Well, better go.' He smiles at us both, then goes to touch me, but I pull away; he grimaces with the half smile, and then lifts a hand and swings out the kitchen door and is gone.

15

I'm making love with Yanni. I'm lying over him, kissing his ears, his cheekbones, the hollows of his throat. He has his hands behind his head and my hair brushes his chest and sides and he laughs throatily. I raise my face to his and he's smiling and his eyelids slant the way I remember them and I lift my hand and open my palm and tiny purple hearts scatter in his hair...

I awake smiling, filled with warmth...then feel the coldness of consciousness wash like a winter wave across me. I may never – should never! – make love with Yanni again. Ever again. I may never touch his mouth, see those eyes slant at me, hear his teased laugh...

The realisation sinks like a stone in my chest.

It's daybreak. Friday, two weeks since I last saw him. And I have made no move to contact him, nor he me.

The sky through the eastern windows is painted in unreal child's colours – powder-pastel purple, a strip of pink, then ash grey. The colours remind me absently of the smell of my year nine art room, of the seductive, heady scent of sprayed aerosol on pastel drawings –

But then suddenly also of a surge of other memories. Of Sister Bernadette's viscous Irish voice coating her sarcasm, her red hand slapping my wrist, her rosary beads clicking impatiently against a desk...of whispering, green-ribboned heads grouped away from me, eyes vixen-slanted...her father's that artist...heathen...surprised they let her come here...

And I am sobered. I shake my head quickly. I am not a social outcast any more. Not now that I have a husband and children, and a secure home...and going with Yanni would wreck all of that. I must not contemplate it. The past is the past – another life – and I have good friends

119

now. Julia next door, and others – women I've met through having babies, at parks and through playgroups, who are tolerant of outsiders. Some who are interested in art. Like Lind, who takes eerie and beautiful photographs in mangrove swamp and has got Mark to make her furniture from its twisted trees. How would Julia and Lind react if they knew about Yanni? Knew that I had betrayed Mark? Gossiping about our husbands – talking about potential lovers – was a far cry from actually doing anything.

Mark. I drop my gaze from the window to him, beside me with his sleeping skin clear as a boy's and his mouth pink and plump in its frame of beard. I think of how Mark looked at me last night as we made love, the things he whispered…

I can't, I think abruptly. I can't see Yanni again. My heart has begun to thump in fright. I can't betray Mark again. Ever.

It's a pattern of thought I have repeated over and over since I last saw Yanni.

Today, I think, blinking quickly, I'll go see Lind. Haven't seen her for ages. Make plans with her for the weekend. She's broad-grinned, warm, occasionally vulgar – just what I need to distract me. The children love to play together and love her place: a whitewashed, sandy house with mangroves and the sea behind the giant leaves in her garden. We all like each other, enjoy each other's company. And I haven't rung Peri yet, haven't made any arrangements I have to cancel. And when I do, I won't contact Yanni.

I'm back from Lind's just in time to pick up Ross from school. Then we go grocery shopping and I have to buy new shoes for Charlotte and new shorts for Ross – and by the time we arrive home again, it's half-past five and Mark's ute is parked in the steep driveway.

I honk the horn and call, 'Hey, Mark! Can you move the car? I've got a boot load of groceries here!'

Then Mark emerges from the garage with a face like a mask and begins to quietly and deliberately approach down the ramp, staring at me.

And everything else seems to suddenly be frozen.

'What's wrong?' I've withdrawn physically into the protection of the car, a wave of dread like cold blood in my veins.

He stops two metres away and holds up a creased sheet of paper. 'This is what's wrong.' He flicks it at me and it flutters gently onto the driveway. His eyes are filled with pain and despair, fleetingly: and then with the emptiness of hatred.

I get out of the car, with the engine still running. I pick up the letter. I read,

Just a quick note to thank you for a wonderful time. I just wanted to let you know how happy you made me feel. xxx
    J.

I stare after Mark's back in bewilderment. It looks like a T. Or maybe an F. Not a Y. And Yanni's Ys are not like that anyway. Who do I know whose name starts with T or F? 'Mark, I don't know who this is any more than you do – where did you get it? Where did it come from?'

He yells over his shoulder, his voice like a dog's in his anger. 'I was cleaning up. It was in an envelope with your name on the front. In a pile of junk mail. Don't tell me you don't know who it is!'

'Mark, come on.' I can hear the pleading in my own voice. 'It's an F. Isn't it an F? I don't know anyone we've had over recently…'

'How happy you made me feel?'

'Mark!'

But he's stomping off to the shed, taking the weight painfully still on his damaged leg and I'm left staring up at his back, frozen.

T? F? There's no one I know…

And then I see Julia's signature in my head and I remember how she signs her name and that her 'Js' are flowery, Edwardian –

'Mark!' I cry, running after him. 'Mark! It's Julia. Julia! Mark!'

But it's too late. The shed door is closed and I can hear the buzz of the welder. I slump and turn away.

I know what this means. This means probably a week of anger, of silence, of his working late and growling at the children and ignoring me. Of not even allowing me to get Julia over and have her tell him herself that she wrote the note. Of being back in the pattern again, the cycle of jealousy and forgiveness, the pattern we repeat like a clockwork song every time something presses the button. Until neither of us can stand it any longer and we fight and yell and clear things up.

And he can't see it. He can't see that his ignoring me and his passive fury with me are what drive me to seek the attention of others. The company of others. The memory of others.

After a while, I turn back to the car. The children are still sitting in it, waiting for me to park it somewhere properly, since it's standing on the footpath driveway, purring. I get in and change gears and back out and park on the road, then begin to unload everything from children to groceries to parcels of new shoes and clothes to empty milkshake containers. And I go through the motions of putting things away and helping Ross with his homework and preparing dinner and eating it and bathing bodies and cleaning teeth and reading stories; and I can't even be bothered trying to tell Mark who wrote the note.

When the children are in bed and he has finished the dishes, Mark stomps off up to his shed again, and I sit quietly in the semi-darkness of my room. I find an old photograph of Yanni and I stare and stare at it; and then I search in my handbag for the card I dropped in there. I slip the photograph inside my pillowcase and hold the pillow tight against my chest and then I go into the kitchen and pick up the telephone.

16

It is Friday again, and Charlotte and I are booked on the six o'clock water taxi. Ross is happily at a sleepover at a friend's until tomorrow afternoon when Mark can pick him up, but I couldn't leave Charlotte. Even for Yanni, I couldn't leave Charlotte. I have never spent a night away from her since she was born: never.

Mark has hardly spoken a word to me – he's worked until eight each night and is up at dawn. Before I left, I told him abruptly that I was going to visit Peri again because Aunt Dem wants me to; and I left instructions about where and when to pick up Ross. And told not a lie, after all.

I stand with Charlotte and our bags on the tarmac at Cleveland, both of us with our hands in the pockets of our matching waterproof coats; Charlotte presses her back into my legs. There's a strong wind blowing in from the bay and every so often a gust of light rain brushes us to shelter under the booking office awning. The other passengers are mainly weekend surfers, if the boards under their arms are anything to go by, and a few of what look like locals, probably in 'town' on shopping trips.

The water taxi is a big hovercraft, fully sealed. Even so, the carpet is wet and there is water under the back seats, the ones I choose to sit in so Charlotte has a view of the boat's wake. I put our bags on the seat beside me, on the ticket collector's advice.

'Bit rough out there!' he says, his face wrinkled and sunburned.

I look out and there are some white caps, but it looks safe enough. But it is rough. The rain gets heavier and heavier as we proceed, and the boat lurches alarmingly on the waves so that water sloshes over our shoes. Spray spatters against the oily glass along with the rain. I watch with Charlotte the churned backwash splitting like the Red Sea was supposed to, to allow Moses to lead his people to the Promised Land. And I have a sudden surge of excitement – partly in anticipation of seeing Yanni again, but partly too because I can see the mainland recede.

Yanni is waiting for us with a coat held over his head at the end of the dark, rain-dashed jetty leading from the water taxi to the island. I'm half-carrying Charlotte and lugging our bags as well, so at first he doesn't recognise me – then I see a slight shock jolt him as he does.

'Hi,' I say, a little anxiously, raising my voice above the gusts of rain. 'Sorry – I had to bring Charlotte. Sharlie, do you remember Yanni?'

She lifts her angelic face to his uncertain one, and frowns. Then, 'Yes,' she says solemnly.

Yanni's face relaxes then, into the smile I have always loved so well, and his earring glints in the jetty light. 'That makes two of us,' he says.

I draw a breath of relief. He takes the bags from me and bends to touch my face with his as he does so: his lashes brush my cheek. We bundle into his car – an old but clean station wagon – and in the sudden cocoon of warmth and shelter and quiet I feel how hard my heart is thudding.

'Hell of a weekend to come over! You get too wet?' He's turned to Charlotte in the back, who's sitting up straight, saucer-eyed, her wet fringe slicked across her forehead.

'No,' she says. 'Can we go to the beach now?'

Yanni and I both laugh, and I relax a bit. Yanni starts the car and brushes my knee as he changes gear, and I don't pull away; I glance shyly at him in the light of passing street lamps. His profile is like a movie star's and his hair gleams palely as the lights move over it.

We've agreed to go to my grandmother's house. It's private, and roomy, and besides that filled with shared memories.

'I brought some things to eat,' I say. 'I'm not sure whether the fridge still works or not. We can get fresh milk and things from the corner shop tomorrow, anyway.'

Yanni flashes his eyes at me. 'Stop being a mother,' he says, grinning. 'I've got everything under control. Even the music.' He presses the cassette player button and softly the Hunters and Collectors, a group I associate with the very end of our affair, begin to sing 'Throw Your Arms Around Me'.

I listen to the music and watch in the wing mirror the past and the future existing simultaneously: the road reflected in the mirror transposed against the road ahead.

The generator kicks in as reliably as it always has. Charlotte is tired and hungry despite her insistence on swimming right now; I give her a chicken sandwich and some milk and a warm bath – the hot water system is run by gas – and she cuddles her toy pony and goes off to sleep in my old bed, with the promise of the beach first thing in the morning.

When I come out of her room, I see Yanni has turned off the lounge room lights and is flaming candles.

'Fridge is working,' he says.

He's moved my grandmother's glass-topped dining table from its traditional spot near the kitchen bench over to the darkened lounge room windows. The faded curtains are drawn back, and when he places the candles on the table, the rain beading and running down the glass looks like mercury. There's a plate of cheese and a Greek salad and an open bottle of Hermitage on a clean cloth, and our places are set. Yanni is frying what smells like fish, and there is a line of little bottles beside the stove, which he works his way through one by one. He looks relaxed and comfortable, the sleeves of his jumper pushed up to his elbows and his hands working expertly. I sink into one of the brown velveteen chairs at the table in the candlelight and pour some wine and sip it, watching him. This is a Yanni I haven't seen before: this domestic, confident…man.

'I didn't know you could cook.'

He cocks an eyebrow at me, pausing his measuring from one of the bottles. 'With Mum for a mother?'

I smile. I had forgotten about her dinners: the dolmathakias she'd grow her own vine leaves and mint to make, her golden baked moussaka, her papoutsakia – stuffed eggplant – which looked more like clogs than their 'little shoes' translation, her skewered souvlakia and fish baked with

125

lemon and garlic and oregano – *psari plaki*. The years Yanni and his parents spent in Greece left a lasting legacy of these foods in their lives.

Because my mother is half-Greek, my parents were often invited to Yanni's for meals when we were over on holidays: we children were usually left with my grandmother, who shuddered away from any but the blandest food; but we would get to taste leftovers nevertheless, and I loved to curl the names of the various dishes around my tongue, perhaps remembering dimly the voice of my Greek grandmother, who died when I was small. She had held onto her culture after she and my Italian grandfather immigrated to Australia after the war, and my own mother used to bake traditional Greek dishes on occasions; but Mum saw herself much more as an Australian than a Greek, and, despite my father's delight in Greek cooking, adopted Dad's Anglo-Saxon culture much more readily.

'Well, Mum could cook too, but it didn't mean she taught me.'

Yanni flips the fish, then throws a glance at me again. 'Taste the cheese. It's made locally. Goat's milk.'

I cut a wedge and drop it onto my tongue. It's a moist feta, with a slightly lemony flavour. 'Goats. Don't tell me. Someone's starting to grow olives and figs over here too.' I chew, grinning. 'Before you know it, there'll be tavernas with retsina libations spilt on their stone floors and plate smashing.'

Yanni raises an eyebrow and screws a lid back on a bottle. 'Are you mocking me?'

'*Moi?*'

I sip the wine again, enjoying its heat in my belly, the way it makes me begin to relax, begin to feel happy and at home again in the familiar house with its unfamiliar candlelight. We were always happy, Yanni and I, when we were together here on the island: flirtatious and happy – an edge of sexuality there when we were older, which changed things of course; but nevertheless, comfortable with each other.

'Mocking you, oh Greek hero?'

He places a lid on the frying pan and turns the heat down. He comes over and sits opposite me and stretches out his legs to rest them against mine. His body is as cleanly curved as a comma and his face in the candlelight is like a Picasso painting: the planes seem interlocked, made from something more rigid than flesh. He smiles, and his eyes glitter like water. 'Remember those games we used to play? You and Luke and me? Then just you and me. Those Greek fantasy games.'

I'm nodding, smiling. 'Mum was half-Greek. But you knew all the stories.'

He nods and pours some wine, then pauses, his fingers cupping the bowl of his glass. 'You've kept it, haven't you? This fascination with Greece. Greek myths. The Archilles Heels – at the party.'

I shrug and smile still, a little embarrassed. 'Maybe. Haven't you?'

I watch him hesitate, not looking at me; then he shrugs too, and sips the wine.

'Yanni?' I say.

He moves his legs abruptly away from mine then, and tucks them under his chair. He fiddles with a silver ring on his left pinkie and purses his lips, then meets my gaze. 'Well – no, not really. I mean, I cook Greek because I like it and I can do it and –' he grins lopsidedly – 'it's pretty impressive, you've got to admit! But…umm, I dunno: the myths seem pretty stupid, really, when you think about them.' He pushes the sleeves of his jumper up his arms again, and, and watches me. He shrugs. 'I dunno. I suppose I was just wondering why you still – you know.' And he looks at me, questioningly.

I stare at him, and am silent for a moment. Then I say deliberately, 'Because they remind me of you.'

He can't mistake my meaning. I watch him. He nods, but I can't read his expression.

After a minute, he says abruptly, leaning back, 'You took a long time to call me.'

I look down and push hair behind my ear. 'I didn't know what to do.'

He is silent.

'I still don't.'

Silence again. Then he abruptly leans towards me and places his hand on mine, and he's frowning and his eyes are suddenly dark with intensity. 'Ven,' he says, 'Ven, don't...don't...'

I look at him blankly, confused.

Then his face relaxes and his hand curls unsteadily from mine. 'Sorry,' he says. 'Forget it. Leave it. It's nothing. Uh! The fish!'

I stare after him in bewilderment. My heart beats a little too fast. 'Yanni?' I say, when he comes back with steaming plates.

He pauses, standing beside me, holding the dishes. And then he smiles – his radiant smile, the smile that lights up his eyes and makes them flash in the candlelight like jewels. 'Don't worry about it.' His voice is casual again, offhand. 'It's nothing. Now – is this like my mother's fish, or what?'

We eat, and drink the wine, then some more of another bottle. We talk about ourselves. I don't mention Mark, or the children, even though their names spring to my tongue twenty times at least; and he tells me about his surfing career and his surf shop on the island.

'That's where you met Peri again, wasn't it? She came in to buy a boogie board?' I say suddenly. She's been on my mind – I have no idea what I'm going to say to her tomorrow – what I should say to her. But I'm curious about his relationship with her too.

'Peri?' He looks suddenly wary.

I lift an eyebrow at him. 'Yes, Peri – my cousin.'

He grins uncertainly. 'Oh, that Peri. Mmm.'

I watch him carefully. 'She was pretty taken with you.'

He holds my gaze, then smiles and shrugs. 'She's pretty taken with a few people, from the look of it.'

My heart turns over. My breath quickens. He's avoided my implied question. 'You mean Haden.'

'Uh-huh.' He puts his glass down and starts stacking our plates, scraping the fish bones together.

I gulp some wine, and go on unsteadily, 'He met her the first day she arrived – he almost ran into her. In his car.'

'Did he?' He sounds uninterested.

'So what do you think of Haden?' I force him to look at me.

He's about to get up, take the dishes to the sink; but he pauses, looking at my face. Then he puts the plates down and sits again, and I can see he's relieved that I've changed the subject. His voice when he speaks is relaxed and confident again. 'Well, I don't know anything for sure – don't know him personally, though I've met him of course – you meet everyone here eventually. But there are rumours. He's loaded: there's always rumours about the loaded. He imports coke, ecstasy – picks them up on his yacht or couriers them. That's one story. He's got a management job in the mine, but that doesn't earn him enough to buy the property he has over here. And to let that house right on the water to Peri rent-free.' He says the last with a twist of his mouth.

'So everybody knows about that?' I'm relieved too, to be on this topic, on neutral ground. Somewhere in my brain I'm anxious about what has not been said about Peri, but juggling with Haden, with him as the problem, is much more comfortable.

He shrugs again.

'But what about Peri? Haden and Peri? What's going on there? And the drugs – Aunt Dem's heard, God know who from…' I trail off, wondering then if I should mention the bruises I saw on Peri's wrist as well; but I shy away from bringing her up again.

He looks back at me then, and his eyes gleam and glitter, large and luminous, in the candlelight and the beading rain; and what he says loosens that knot of anxiety in my belly. 'I think,' he says, slowly, 'Haden's got it bad. Seen him with her. He's careful – doesn't show too much – but he's got it bad.' He seems surprised at his own insight. 'As for the drugs, who knows? Leave that to the cops.'

I'm silent. I suddenly remember the car I thought I'd heard pulling up outside her place the Friday night I spent with her. Was that Haden, hoping she'd be alone? I think, oh, if only that's so. If only he does love her; if only she loves him back…so long as drugs aren't involved…

'It's strange, isn't it?' Yanni's picked up a stray knife and is sliding it gently between his fingers, frowning. 'You don't see men go for women like that so much. I mean, men want success…women are just part of the deal. The spoils. Not for him, though. He's got it all – money, success… And yet he looks at her…'

I sit quite still, and stare at him: and the knot in my belly is as tight again as a clenched fist. It's like that for you, isn't it? I want to say. The surfing success has always been the most important thing to you. I'm – a hundred other women probably – unimportant. I feel a wrench, a split, as of a chasm silently opening in the ground between us. Stop, I think, stop, change the subject, joke…don't go there, not even in your head. Make the most of this – enjoy it, live in the moment…like he does. He invited you here. You. And he's made this lovely meal, and he's accepted Sharlie. And he's told you he loves you. It's enough.

'Ven?' I look up quickly: he's watching me, a half smile on his face, his earring catching the candlelight. 'You okay?'

'What? Oh! Sorry.' I relax, smiling. 'Just thinking about Peri.' I stand up. 'I'll get these dishes out of the way. That was wonderful. Thank you – for all of it.'

He smiles lazily and leans back. 'My pleasure, my love.'

That word again.

While I'm doing the dishes, Yanni moves to the couch. He flicks on a lamp above it, and stretches out. He watches me, and smiles. 'Hurry up with that. It could wait until the morning…'

'Nearly done.' I swab the bench tops quickly.

He moves his legs and I sit beside him on the couch. He puts his arm around me and begins to kiss me

And I hear Charlotte cry.

He continues to kiss me, but I freeze. I draw back. He lets me go reluctantly.

'I won't be a minute,' I whisper.

I take Charlotte to the toilet, then settle her in bed again.

When I come back, Yanni is sitting up, watching the rain on the window, his hands clasped between his knees. He smiles at me faintly as I drop down beside him again. He goes to say something, then stops. He wraps me with his arm again, and he whispers into my hair, 'Oh Ven, Ven, you must know…'

My heart flutters. Go on, I think, speak. Tell me you love me again, tell me you have loved me all these years, and I will leave Mark. Without a doubt. Despite what I've gone over in my head, despite the selfishness of it, despite the fact that that is the wrong decision…

But he's not going to tell me that. Is he? I crouch silently within the circle of his arm and will him to speak.

The rain crackles gently against the windows and on the tin roof.

He bends his forehead to mine, and I can smell the wine and fish on his breath; but when he speaks his voice is such a low murmur that I can hardly catch it. 'Tonight, you belong to me again.'

But when I look up, startled, I see that he isn't smiling. He looks, if anything, sad.

17

At three o'clock in the morning, I awake from my second nightmare. Earlier, I dreamed I was at home; a man arrived on my doorstep claiming he owned the house and giving me a summons saying he was bankrupt and I owed him four thousand dollars. I woke and realised it was a dream; I curled into Yanni and went back to sleep. Then I dreamed I was on the Metro in Paris with Ross. I was reading the summons and trying to work it out. Ross became impatient with me and said he wanted to go back to Mark and Charlotte. I said sure, and he got off at the next stop. I relaxed in the peaceful train, then suddenly realised I didn't know at which station he had left – then I didn't know where the train I was on was going. I panicked, got off, couldn't find which train went back – I started in horror, imagining Ross lost, with no one speaking English, and with him not knowing where we were staying. Then I became confused: I realised I must be dreaming because in reality I would never allow Ross to leave by himself. But the summons seemed to make sense, and I thought then maybe the second dream was reality as well…

The nightmare shakes me unbearably, but the relief of knowing it is a dream is even stronger. I sit up wide-eyed in the darkness, my heart thumping, staring at but not seeing the black shape of the house next door through the bedroom window.

Then I do see, because a light flicks on in that house. I watch a man and a woman move into a picture frame of light. The woman carries a baby: she bends and places the baby tenderly in what must be a cradle under the window. Long dark hair swings and obscures her face. Her shoulder dips out of sight. The man, balding and tender-faced, stands beside her, watching. Then they turn and smile at each other and leave the room. The light dims.

And my mouth is filled with a sadness that tastes like grief.

Despite, or perhaps because of, the nightmare, I rise early, moving quietly so I don't wake Yanni. I check on Charlotte: always a late riser, she's still asleep, her eyelids long and smooth, her mouth all soft peaks and languid lines. I pull on my running shoes and sprint out along paths as familiar to me as the scent of the banksias and the hush of the sand. The rain has quite gone and the air is almost motionless.

I stop at the local shop on the way back: it has a phone booth outside. I dig out the coins I slipped in my sock and phone Peri. As I expect, I get the answering machine: Haden's legacy – the reason Aunt Dem can't get through to Peri.

'Hi, Peri,' I say. 'It's Ven. I'm over for the weekend again, with Sharlie. I'm staying at Gran's.'

There's a series of beeps and then Peri's voice cuts in. She sounds bleary and croaky. 'Ven? What the hell are you doing here?'

'I…' I'm taken aback.

'Shit! It's bloody Mum, isn't it? Mum's sent you over.'

'No! Well, she is – worried… Look,' I say hurriedly, 'can I meet you today? Can I come over?'

There's a silence. Then, 'Yes. Yes, that would be – good. Actually, there're some things I want to – get your opinion on, anyway. Some things have happened… What time?'

'After lunch? One-thirty or so?'

I hear her swallowing, then the clink of a glass. 'Okay.'

Charlotte and Yanni are both still asleep when I get back. I make hot, sweet tea and take some in to Yanni, as my grandmother used to do to Shelley and me and Luke; he doesn't stir, so I leave it by the bed. By then, Charlotte is awake, sleepy-eyed and pink-cheeked; she sits on the floor in the bathroom with a cup of warm milk, chirping excitedly about sandcastles and waves while I fill the bath for myself with the tea-coloured bore water she'd never seen till yesterday.

And I wonder, as I did last time I was here, why I never made the effort to bring my children back here. Was it only because I shied away from the effort of disrupting babies' routines and the worry about disturbing my dying grandfather? Or was it also because the memory of Yanni had become an obsession? That it was okay to bring Mark here, on our honeymoon, to the place where I had experienced an epiphany of happiness, because we, too, were happy then... But not to touch that nerve of rejection, once Mark started rejecting me? Not to contaminate memory.

Yanni sleeps late. By the time he joins us on the beach – what there is left now the channel has gnawed into so much of it – it's almost ten o'clock.

'Hi,' I say shyly. I daren't reveal too much in front of Charlotte; plus I don't know how he'll react to me.

He flops down beside me with his brown arms smooth and silky against the yellow of his T-shirt, and his legs long and tanned and gold-furred. 'Thanks for the tea.'

'Must have been cold.'

'Yeah. Drank it anyway.' He's looking at me, smiling a little, his eyes the exact colour of the shallows; my reflection swims in them.

'I had nightmares. About the children.' I shudder still at the memory. Suddenly I long for him to wrap me in his arms, reassure me, tell me everything will work out, there's nothing to be afraid of, as long as we love each other... But I've made it clear he mustn't touch me in front of Charlotte, and love can't solve any of my nightmares, any of my fears.

He looks at my daughter, who's digging a moat around her sandcastle, just as she's seen Ross do. 'I can imagine,' he says, gently. Then he sits up, briskly. 'Hey, Charlotte – you been looking for stingrays yet?'

'Stingrays?' She raises her head from her work, her eyes saucers again.

'Sure. I think we can still get by here on this tide. Come on.'

'Only if Mummy comes.'

'Of course,' I say.

We thread our way north along the eroded beach, through the shallows which wash against dead and half-dead trees: against tea trees, percolating into the sea, flecking the water with debris like tea leaves and seeping a stain like sin into it; against red mangroves, their roots tangled like hair in the water and their branches dipped resignedly in the salt. There is a scent of eucalyptus – sharp and stingy – a scent that reminds me of the sound of cicadas. The shallows are the colour of pale green glass, the channel beyond navy blue, and the sky as clean and smooth as a wild duck's egg.

We pass Yanni's old house: he tells me his mother sold it long ago. It is closed and silent.

We don't find any stingrays and we don't see any dolphins, but we do find other treasures: dredged shells, ropey seaweed and a coconut full of milk. Charlotte of course falls into the water; but the sun is warm and she gasps and laughs and falls in again and it becomes a game. Then Yanni pretends to trip and fall in too – Charlotte squeals with delight and paddles after him. I hesitate; then I stash the treasures and the towel I've brought in the fork of a tree and dive in as well.

It's cold, but not icy as the channel would be; and it's so clean and shallow it's like being in the children's wading pond at the local swimming pool. The suck and hush of the waves against the eroded land is curiously soothing and almost sexual.

We frolic in the water as if all of us are children, and I allow Yanni to touch me under the water and to kiss me when Charlotte isn't looking. We move closer and closer to the channel, but I'm aware of it all the time, and I steer Charlotte back. For me, it's always been a potent force, a dark underbelly of water lurking with sharks and stingrays and bottomless cold currents – a dangerous underworld on the edge of a children's playground. I've only ever once kicked over the edge – that day I first seduced Yanni; and even though Yanni dives into it now suddenly, perhaps remembering that other time too, I ignore him and turn back to my little daughter paddling so proudly in the golden-green sun-streaked lagoon.

At midday, we dry off and turn back to the house.

18

I park my grandmother's rusty, unregistered Mini, abandoned in Serenity's garage when she moved to the mainland, on the road above Peri's place, and glance down: but the foliage seems even more overgrown, and the mottled silver of the house roof is barely distinguishable. I unstrap Charlotte, straighten her clothes and take her hand. She clutches her pony, as usual, in the other.

This time, we don't go to the front door. We follow the trail around to the back, around to the cliff. Charlotte follows me dutifully up the warm splintery stairs, and holds my hand as I knock on the door and peer through the glass wall from the deck.

There is no answer. I hesitate. I curse myself for not having tried the front: Charlotte's legs are small and slow, so I'll probably have to carry her back up there. I can hardly leave her on a child-unfriendly deck.

But when I turn to her, she's already starting down the steps. And I see what she has spied: a shift of white sand banked against a sturdy gum tree. She moves purposely toward it.

She can never get enough of sand. I watch her sit and prop her pony carefully in it, then trickle it through her fingers, dreamily. She is like me, I think suddenly. A person who lives through her senses – for whom touch and taste and sound and smell are as potent as sight to her imagination, to a world she much prefers to the real one. Maybe, I think, that's where the word 'sensitive' comes from...

'Ven.' Peri's voice startles me, coming at the same time as the French door unlocking. 'Hi. Sorry – I was upstairs – come in. How are you?' She's kissing my cheek, taking my hand: her familiar gestures of welcome, her whiff of shampoo and musk-scented perfume as familiar. But there is something different: although she is casually dressed in muslin and shells, she no longer looks thin and nervous. Her face has a healthy tan, and the edginess I sensed last time I met her here is gone.

'Good, good!' I return her kiss and smile but hang back from the house. 'Charlotte's down there…'

Peri moves to the railing of the deck. 'Hi, Sharlie!'

Charlotte looks up and smiles. Her social skills are developing, maybe thanks to Aunt Dem and her treats, or even to Peri's hot chocolate and potato straws from last time.

Peri turns back to me. 'I'll make some coffee: we can have it out here, where you can keep an eye on her.'

'Thanks.' I smile. 'She's unlikely to wander off, but you never know.'

I lean on the deck rail and look out at the sea when Peri has gone back inside. It is a stunning aquamarine today, gently moving as if from sleeping breaths, with only ruffles of wind to shiver its skin. There are no boats that I can see, and the sandbank is submerged. On the far horizon, to the east, grey clouds blossom like giant, overblown flowers.

Peri comes back with cups and a full plunger, and we sit at the table where we had lunch three weeks ago, after my visit to Serenity with the children. In my peripheral vision, I can see that Charlotte is still playing with the sand: she's tired probably, since I have wrecked her afternoon sleep routine again, but happy so far.

'Well…where do I start?' She pulls a packet of cigarettes from a pocket of her dress and lights one. She smirks at my astonishment. 'Taken it up temporarily. Don't look so worried!'

I grimace. 'Sorry. Okay…well, how about with what's going on with Haden?' I take the plunge. 'With the rumours about him being involved with drugs? With the bruises I saw on your wrist last time I was here?' I gaze at her challengingly.

She looks at me and raises her eyebrows. 'I…whose rumours?'

'Aunt Dem's heard something, I don't know where. And Yanni.'

Her eyes narrow. 'Yanni? When were you talking to him?'

'I…when I saw him, you know…'

She flicks ash from her cigarette impatiently. 'What would he know? Or Mum? And anyway, if so many people know, then why hasn't he been arrested?'

I'm silent. That has occurred to me too.

Then she sighs. 'Look, tell Mum I'm fine, okay? I'm not going to go using anything dangerous, addictive, if that's what she thinks.' She suddenly grimaces. 'Except the legal things.' She holds up her cigarette to me. I'm starting to smile with relief when she adds, offhand, 'Eccies are not nearly so bad for you.'

'Eccies!'

She smiles then, and I see mischief flash. 'Ecstasy. Cocaine gives you a buzz, but I'm not doing that any more: eccies are much better, all round.'

'Peri!'

'You wanna try one? Greeeat with sex...mmm-mmmm, the best.' She's drawing on her cigarette, her expression smug.

I stare at her in dismay. 'Sex with...Haden?'

She shrugs. 'Who else?'

'But I thought you were keen on Yanni...'

'That bastard?' Her mouth twists. 'Got over him quick smart. No, Haden. Gotta tell you, he's a bloody fantastic lover.' She stubs out her cigarette, and suddenly jumps up. 'Come on, come with me. I want to show you something.'

I don't know what to say, what to think. I glance down at Charlotte, off in a world of her own, innocent and sweet and lovely. And I understand Aunt Dem: I understand her anguish and worry. Her pain. Her helplessness.

'You coming?'

I frown. 'Okay.' I look over the railing and raise my voice. 'Sharlie, I'm just going inside for a moment. You be all right down there?'

She looks up at me and nods, smiling. I follow Peri.

She takes me up the internal stairs, into the gloom above. She fumbles for a key in the pocket of her long muslin dress, and unlocks one of the dark oak doors off the hallway. I follow her in. She moves over to heavy curtains and draws them back. A rectangle of dusty light springs across toffee floorboards, and the room comes into soft focus.

The walls are painted a dark, rich green. A broad bed covered in red satin dominates the room. At its base is a padlocked blanket box. There are long silk scarves tied to the brass bedhead, and on a side table are candles, an indigo pottery vase holding an assortment of artist's paint-brushes, bristles up, an ornate wooden box, a jar of green oil and a translucent purple vibrator in the shape of a thick, veined penis.

I look at Peri, and she's regarding me with amusement. 'This is... the Men's Room. In this room, anything goes.' She taps the toe of her shoe lightly on the blanket box. 'Anything he wants.' Her voice is slow and deep and melodramatic. She drops her sleeves back, and I see there are faint marks on both her wrists. 'We get a bit carried away at times.'

I stare at her. 'And the paintbrushes?' I say faintly.

'Mmm, the feel of that on your skin...lighter than feathers...' She brushes her fingertips over the bristles, then plucks out the broadest one and runs it over the inside of her forearm. She puts it back and picks up the wooden box. She holds it out to me, open. There is a strong scent of camphor – but nothing else. The red velvet interior is empty. Then Peri presses something in the base, and a false bottom springs back, to reveal twenty or so many-coloured pills. 'Eccies. Want to try one?' Her voice is slightly mocking.

I roll my eyes at her. 'Okay. You've made your point. But – are you sure none of this is...dangerous, Peri?'

She shakes her head. 'With eccies, you just have to make sure you drink a lot of water. No more dangerous than certain antidepressants, actually. Many similar properties to antidepressants, in fact. Only an-tidepressants are legal.' She grimaces.

'And...the rest?'

One side of her mouth lifts. 'Ven...I know what I'm doing. It's all just...games.'

I look at her doubtfully. 'If you say so.'

She grins and puts her arm around my shoulder affectionately.

We go back downstairs, in silence.

I check on Sharlie, and Peri comes over to lean on the deck rail beside me. I notice absently that the grey clouds to the east are expanding, and that a breeze has freshened on the ocean.

'You won't tell Mum, though, will you, Ven?' Peri's voice is suddenly clipped. 'About the eccies. Promise?'

I shake my head at her. 'Of course not! What do you take me for?'

She smiles faintly. 'I don't even know why I told you...'

'I do.' I turn to her and lighten my tone. 'You wanted to shock me, or show off! Show me how worldly you are, maybe!'

She wriggles her shoulders, then grins. 'Maybe. Hey, well, if that's my motivation, there's something else I should tell you then!'

'Oh?'

'Haden asked me to marry him. The day before yesterday.'

It's a bombshell. I turn to her, stunned. 'What?'

'Haden has asked me to marry him. Then he wants to take me to America, and try to get me an agent. For the paintings. He thinks they're really good. What do you think I should do?'

'But...wow, Peri, that's fantastic!' I stand still, staring at her – then grab her, hug her. 'Fantastic! Wow. What do you mean, what should you do? You're kidding, aren't you!' My voice is high-pitched with surprise.

She purses her lips, half a frown and half a smile on her face. 'Well, I know. I mean, I really like him...he's rich and exciting – interested in me... But, well, America. It's a long way from Mum. And despite everything...'

I shake my head, smiling. 'I knew you were all talk.'

'Yeah.' She grimaces. 'If Haden hadn't been letting me stay here rent-free, I'd probably have gone back to her by now.'

I lower my arms from her gently. 'Have you contacted her yet?'

She shakes her head, then purses her lips again. 'I do love her. I do. And yet, and yet...she relied on me too much. Wanted too much from me. Now she's still trying to run my life. Sending you here – how dare she! You know, there's a man up there – Bob – and I thought if I wasn't around, if she was lonely… Oh, you know.'

I nod.

'But nothing's happened. At least that I've heard, from a friend up there who's keeping an eye out for me. So of course I'm feeling guilty.'

'Look.' I take one of her hands: it's cool and ringless. 'She's worried about you, that's all. She's got her own life, and I'm sure she'd love to hear that you've got yours and that you're happy. I think that's all you have to do. Contact her, and tell her about Haden. Only – maybe not about that room up there…'

We smile at each other.

'Let's finish our coffee,' I say.

Peri makes a new pot. Charlotte comes back up to me while Peri's away: she tucks her pony under an arm and dusts the sand from her fingers as she starts up the stairs. She's sitting on my knee, telling me about the adventures her pony has had on a desert island, when Peri emerges again. This time, she has a plate of Tim-Tams with the coffee. Charlotte's eyes widen.

We talk about Mum, and Aunt Dem for a little, but before long we're back to Haden, and weddings, and America.

Then eventually, when I can drop it into the conversation without being obvious, I say, 'Peri. Earlier, when you were telling me about having a relationship with Haden, you said that Yanni was a bastard. What did he do to you, if you don't mind me asking? Just curious…'

She is silent for a moment, and I see pain cross her face. Then she presses her lips together and glares at me. 'Yanni!'

I shake my head slightly, alarmed. Does she know about us then? But why would she…

Then I realise the glare is an inward one – at him. And I realise her mood has changed for a third time.

'You want to hear his story, Ven? Would you like to hear what your friend does?'

141

'I...'

She flips open her packet of cigarette, picks one out and lights it. 'He fucks up people's lives, that's what he does.' She inhales and breathes out a smoky dragon puff. 'That's why he's going to Sydney. Did you know that he was going to Sydney? He's done the damage here, and now he's moving on. Before it gets too hot, this time. Before he's run out of town. Like he was in Agnes.'

I shake my head at her, my face frozen. 'Agnes?'

'Yeah. Agnes Waters. Little town, up the coast between Gin Gin and Gladstone. Beautiful surfing beach. He was there for a while.'

Yes, I think: he said that day at Southbank that he'd travelled up the coast of Queensland, wherever there was surf...

'Well, he managed to screw up pretty badly there – sex with a minor – no charges – the girl was mad keen, apparently: used to hang around his place and get him to teach her to surf. But the parents were pretty pissed off, and the whole thing was a big scandal for the girl – you know what small towns are like.' She's glaring disgustedly at the sea now. 'You find out things like that, on an island like this. Someone knows someone. The surfing community is pretty incestuous...'

I interrupt her. 'But – she wasn't pregnant or anything?' I have a falling frightening faintness that reminds me of my own early weeks of pregnancy, and the question is hardly more than a mumble.

'Oh no – caught red-handed, though.'

Oh, Yanni, I think, Yanni... I breathe out, and grope blindly for a response. 'But you can't really blame him, can you? I mean, if she wanted it too...he might not even have known how old she was – I mean, to be fair...'

'She was a minor! Ven, come off it! He had to take responsibility – he –'

'Oh yes.' I cut her off hurriedly. 'Yes, yes, you're right, of course... but what's happened, what's happened here?'

'What's happened here?' She looks back at me and her shells clatter. 'Only him trying to move in on me, shying away because of Haden, but all the time having it off with a local girl who's been living with someone for three years. I'm just waiting for Martin to find out – but Yanni's not. No – he's bailing.' Her voice is harsh and finishes with a bitter break. She flicks her cigarette in the ashtray. 'And now – now – get this – there's a rumour that he's got some other woman – really married this time – in Brisbane.'

I stare at her, and swallow, but before I can say anything she continues relentlessly. 'Poor stupid bitch. Hope she knows what she's doing, but I doubt it. You know what pisses me off the most about him, Ven? You know what makes me really angry? That we all fall for it. That's he's able to do it, because we all fall for him. And he just exploits that – he just uses it! He couldn't care less about any of us!'

Oh, no, I think; that not true! Not for me anyway – for the others, okay, they might mean nothing… But not me! I mean something to him! We go back so far – I was his first love – he said last night, as we were making love, that I'm special, beautiful he called me, that he has always cared…

'… I shouldn't have slept with him. God, I could have wrecked everything. It was a stupid thing to do, but you know what he's like. Haden was in Bris – he goes in every Wednesday…'

'What?'

She starts at my tone of voice. 'Haden…went to Brisbane last Wednesday. I… Yanni came round, and you know…' She's frowning at me. 'Ven? Are you okay?'

I stare at her but I can't focus on her. I hold onto Charlotte and breathe shallowly. 'Yanni slept with you last Wednesday?' I say it very carefully and clearly.

'Um. Yeah.' Her expression is still puzzled, and her voice is slightly apologetic. 'I guess I wasn't sure about Haden, where things were going – they do it all the time, don't they?' Her tone changes to defiance. 'So why shouldn't we? Although, perhaps –' her voice is momentarily reflective, and then even a little proud – 'Haden may not be that way. Ven, are you okay? You look quite white.'

I focus on her. Vaguely, I know I have to say something, explain my reaction somehow. 'Sorry,' I mutter. 'I've got my period,' I lie. 'I – just had a bad spasm. Ever since I've borne children, I get really bad pain, at times. I guess the paracetamol must be wearing off.'

'Oh! God – you poor thing. Can I get you some more?' Her voice is full of concern.

'That would be great. Thanks.' My voice is more a whisper than a mutter now. And perhaps, I think dully, it will be good to have some anyway: perhaps it will keep numb the rupture of despair slowly tearing open in my chest.

'Sure.' She hurries away, her white dress fluttering with her movement.

I see Charlotte staring at me, her face worried. Empathy starts early with girls, I register, vaguely.

'Mummy?' she touches my arm tentatively. 'Are you okay, Mummy?'

'Oh, yes, yes, darling!' But my bottom lip has started to tremble: I bite it. 'I'm fine, sweetheart.'

She stares at my wet eyes, frowning. Then she holds out the pony she has clutched in her fist. 'Do you want to borrow Pelly?'

And I wince a smile.

19

When I get back to the house, Yanni isn't there. I put Charlotte down for her sleep and take a chair out to weak winter sun on the edge of the sea. There's a wind rising: I can see white caps forming on the waves far out. There's that bank of cloud moving in from the east, that I saw from Peri's deck. I shiver. I stare at the channel water heaving at the rocks my grandparents bulldozed in to stop the erosion of their land. They stopped the channel: at the brink of their house, almost; but they lost two hundred metres of seafront real estate. And all the cabins my grandfather built by hand, cabins which in the holidays were full of families, and at other times of fishermen, or drunks, or spiders, toppled gradually into the sea. I look out at the ocean. All those memories, I think. All of that, just annihilated.

I look out, but the horizon has blurred.

When I am my rational self again, I think through what Peri has told me. I try to make sense of Yanni: what is real about him; what I know about him from those childhood years; and what Peri, my wayward, explosive, but truthful cousin Peri, has told me.

He's a man with charisma: that is certain. I was his first lover: that is certain. He loved me? Less certain...now. And, in fact, something that was never said when we were young. Which was why, which was why, when he said at my home the day he caught me between the cool white sheets, and arrogantly pressed his mouth over mine – between the cool white sheets I was washing for my husband as well as for myself, I suddenly think, with a bolt of reality again –

Which was why when he said that I loved him and he me, I was pierced with a blade of blinding hope.

I close my eyes. He should not have said it, I think, watching the luminous sky above the grey ocean reverse to negative behind my eyelids: a black sky and a sea pawing whitely at the island. He should not have said it. And he should not last night have told me I'm special and beautiful, if he's been having sex with two other women. If he's been having sex with them, he's been having relationships with those women: whether those women are involved with other men or not...

And then I see the pattern. I see the pattern in the women he chooses. He chooses the unattainable ones. The girl in the three-year relationship; Peri, obviously succumbing to Haden; the young girl in Agnes Waters, impossible as a partner...and me. Me, when I was twenty and two years older than him; and me now, married, with children.

I cover my face with my hands. Did he tell all of those other women, too, that they were special and beautiful? Venny, I think. Oh, Venny. You fool. You stupid, blind fool.

It's while I'm sitting there that Yanni comes back. I hear his car, then wait for him to check for me in the house. I glance back at his easy stride, his thongs squeaking the sand. He comes as if to kiss me, but all my body language rejects him, and he doesn't: perhaps he thinks Charlotte is nearby. I've brought out a chair for him too; I gesture to it with my head.

'How's the shop?' I ask.

He shrugs. 'Fine.' He looks relaxed, happy. He slings one gold-haired leg over the other, and his earring flashes along with his eyes. A black leather thong around his neck makes him look like a tame pussycat. 'Good surf out there today too. Be big by this evening. Maybe too big. Tempting.' He grins at me.

'R-ight.' I drop my eyes then. I look at the sea, at the way the waves flip against the rocks, harmless at the moment. I let my hair mask my face.

'How's Peri?'

'She's...getting married.' My voice is flat. I can feel my lips clammed over the word. I still don't look at him, don't even want to gauge his reaction.

'What?' I can tell from his voice that it is a complete surprise.

'To Haden, of course. They're going to America. He's very keen on her paintings: and he has connections there who might be interested.'

He responds cheerily, with relief, I think; I turn towards him and see he has leaned back in his chair and is looking at the sea.

'But Ven, that's good! Good! Wow, I never… That's great: great! Knew Haden liked her – told you, didn't I? Knew he liked her paintings too – got her to paint the view from his house – the one she's staying in – did you know that?' He looks animated.

'No. How did you know?' And he still doesn't pick up on my clipped tone.

He shrugs, smiling. 'It's a small island. Know someone who knew Ruth, the girl Peri was flatting with. Peri was excited about the commission.'

'Her paintings are good,' I say. 'And she'll be a hit, particularly with the people Haden has promised to show her work to. I'm…happy for her.'

Neither of us says anything for a minute. I sense his disquiet at my obvious tension. I take a breath, then catch his eye. 'Yanni, tell me something. Truthfully. Would you ever have contacted me again? If you hadn't run into me at that party?'

He's a bit taken aback by the abruptness of the question, but he takes it in his stride. He meets my eye, and half-smiles, quizzically. Then he ducks his chin so all I can see is a soft bleached fall of hair; he clasps his hands loosely between his knees. 'I wanted to, Ven.'

'Did you?'

He looks up, and his lovely wide-apart sea eyes beneath the flopped blond hair are filled with sincerity. 'Ven, you are special to me. You were the first – there's always something special about the first, isn't there? And it was all so…intense. And I've thought of you: I've thought of you a lot over the years…you're a very sexy woman…'

'So you said last night.' I watch him.

'And I always thought that one day I'd like to get back together…' His voice peters out, less certain now. He looks down at the sand, his hands clasped. Then he meets my eye again and says slowly, 'But Ven, you were married.'

'I still am.' I fling the words at him. 'So what's changed?'

'Venny? What's the matter?' He draws back, startled.

'Come on, Yanni – be truthful. Can you be truthful with me, please?'

'Truthful?'

'Yes. Truthful. Tell me if I mean anything to you, or if this is just a pleasant weekend for you, before you head off, out of my life again. Tell me if you meant it when you said you loved me. Tell me why you left eleven years ago, without saying goodbye!'

'Hey, hey, Ven – hush! Calm down, honey... You don't want to wake the baby!' He pulls his chair towards me across the sand and rubs my shoulder, trying to make me smile. But I glare at him, and he grimaces ruefully. 'Ven – don't spoil it...'

'Spoil it!'

He withdraws his hand then, and intertwines his fingers between his knees, looking down. He's quiet.

'Tell me. Tell me why you left without saying goodbye.'

'All right.' He sighs. 'I was going to tell you anyway...just waiting for the right moment. Guess this is it, hey?' He smiles weakly. Then he turns to the ocean, and I watch hesitation, and something darker, flutter across his face. I watch him close his eyes and look down again. Then those eyes, those wide-set sea-green eyes, flash at me, and he says slowly, 'Because I thought you might be my sister.'

'What? What?' I stare at him in shock. I feel confusion, fear, panic, tremble on the edge of my consciousness. I shake my head. 'No. No! It's not true! You're lying!' I struggle to regain control.

And, incredibly, he nods. His face is solemn, and he's nodding and shaking his head at the same time. 'It's not true. You're not my sister. But at the time – I just – I saw something between your mum and my dad, and thought about your hair, so blonde, and you remember that note your mother left you... I hope to God you're using something... and I just put two and two together...'

I'm shaking my head, staring at him, even though I'm remembering Aunt Dem's words about my mother…she nearly left him once…she told me, no one else…

'But you're right: I was wrong. I just jumped to conclusions, that's all. But at the time I had to get away. Get away from…'

And I know he means me. I take two deep breaths. Calm down, I think: calm down. Try to keep all of this in your head. Don't panic. 'So how did you find out you were wrong?'

He shrugs. 'I asked Dad.'

'And he said no.'

'He said that he had had a brief fling with your mother, but it was ages after you were born.' And he says it staring down at the debris-flecked white sand.

A brief fling, I think. Exactly the same sort of fling you are having with me. Like father like son; like mother, like daughter. For surely my mother must have been in love with his father, to have risked everything –

'By the time I asked him, it was too late. You had met Mark, and you had your own world, and I didn't belong in it.' He's looking at me as if this explains everything, as if I am just going to accept this, and we write it off as tragic history and we get on with our lives. Or he does.

'Yanni,' I say flatly, 'that's not the reason you left. Or at least, not the only reason. Because you would have told me.' I make my voice soft. 'Wouldn't you?'

He lowers his head again, and I watch his nostrils flaring as he breathes. I watch a pinched whiteness appear at the corners of his nose and a faint pink spot I have never seen before forming at its tip. And, to my surprise, I see a small patch of thinning hair on the blonde crown of his head.

He looks up at me and sighs. 'Ven…'

'Yes?'

'I was eighteen. I wanted to…experience things. Is that so bad?'

'I wouldn't have stopped you. I just didn't understand…'

'No. I should have explained. I'm sorry.'

We both look at the sand, then I shrug acceptance. I say quietly, 'I would have waited for you. If you'd asked me to.' I can see him struggling with something. But before he can speak, I say, 'That still doesn't explain why you rang me this time. Why you contacted me, after that party... Why I'm here, now.'

'Oh, well...' He looks up and his expression is more assured. 'That's because something happened to me, the day after that party.'

I watch him distrustfully. 'What happened?'

He lifts an eyebrow and shrugs. He looks out to sea again. 'I went for a surf. Frenchman's Beach. The surf was big, but not huge. It's been bigger. But this time I nearly lost it, missed my timing, crunched my head on the sand. There are freak sandbars around there: when there's a strong rip, sand gets shifted around, from Deadman's and Cylinder. But the waves are great there, when the wind's right... Anyway. I nearly drowned.' His face has tensed, his mouth pulled into a straight line.

I nod slightly. 'And?'

'And you were in my head, Venny! As I was drowning, you were in my head. And when I got out of it, I thought, I have to see you again, be with you again...that's all...' His face is pulled into a parody of a smile: his dimples show, but his eyes are sad.

I stare at him and I have an overwhelming urge to put my arms around him then, to let the rest of it go, to just live for the moment again, without consequences...and then I remember Peri's words: there's a rumour that he's got some other woman – really married this time – in Brisbane... Poor stupid bitch...

I draw a deep breath. 'I know about Peri, Yanni. She told me. I know about the other girl you've been having it off with over here, too.' My voice is slow and clear. We stare at each other. 'I don't understand, Yanni. I don't understand how you can say I'm special to you, when you can go and sleep with other women, when you knew I was coming over this weekend – you invited me...'

'What, and you didn't sleep with your husband, Ven?' He flings his head up with the question, and I'm startled, but I ignore it.

'I've risked everything for you. I've come here, despite my guilt, despite everything – because I love you, Yanni. I love you.'

He stares at me, and I watch the anger slowly fade from his face.

'Ven,' he says, his voice softening, 'look. I love you too. You know that. You're a very attractive woman. But it can't work. You know, you're married, you've got kids...'

'It happens all the time. Divorce...' But even as I say the word, I realise... Oh, God, I think, don't! Stop! Because I can read the expression in his eyes.

'Ven.'

I am silent.

'Ven...look. It'd never work. I'm just not made like that. I can't take on your kids, be a father...' His voice is soft, cajoling.

'But you were so good with Charlotte this morning...'

'Oh, I can play, Ven! I can play with other people's kids – but Ven, taking them on is different.' He sits up and runs his fingers through his hair then drops his hands between his knees again. 'I thought – I thought about it, this morning...but it wouldn't work, Ven. I don't want that. Maybe in ten years...but now... I'm sorry. I love you, and I'll treasure this weekend forever – but you have a your own world, and...I can't belong in it.' He says the last very gently, his eyes very steady, a slight frown between them, his lovely mouth firm.

I lower my head. I nod. I know that it's true. But even so, even so, some stupid myth in my head wants everything to turn out. Wants there to be a happy ending. Wants everything resolved. Wants him to say that he loves me and nothing else matters...now.

Wants him to just love me, no matter what...

'I don't belong in it.'

We are silent for I don't know how long. Time seems irrelevant, drifting, as it does when you have a fever, or have been awake all night, in a hospital, for instance, with a sick child, and you're waiting for the doctor to revisit in the morning, to tell you everything is back to normal and you can go home.

But normal is not what I want. At least, not now. Normal is the last thing I want.

Eventually, when I haven't said anything, when I've given him no response, only the curtain of my hair so he can't see my face, I hear him move. I hear sand shuffle and his chair creak.

And he says, 'Come on, honey. Let's go inside. Make the most of it…'

And something inside me snaps. I begin to feel the blood rising in my arteries, filling my chest. I think, I'm going to knock him off his chair. How dare he do this to me? Lure me here, offer to pick me up in his car so I'm dependent on him, feed me food and wine and candllight, tell me he loves me? He, and Mark: they don't understand the word. Desire, that's all they feel – desire – and when they're done with that, you're nothing more than an ornament, than someone to clean up after them, than someone to raise their children or their self-esteem…

I look at the waves heaving against the rocks, and at the wind whipping white caps in jittery, restless peaks on the water. I turn back and feel my own breath heaving. 'Yanni…there's something else.'

He looks at me with his eyebrows furrowed – and even though I can feel fury building inside me, even though I'm beginning to hate him, to detest and despise him, I can't look away from the beautiful colour of those eyes. They are the exact colour of the sea, when it is clean and green and innocent, in sunlight – but what they hide, I think then, is just as treacherous, just as dangerous, as what lies beneath the skin of the ocean. I watch him raise a hand and push the hair back from his forehead, as if to erase the puzzle.

'I know…what happened at Agnes Waters.'

And I watch his face transform. I watch him lose it.

He flings his head up and his expression makes my heart contract. 'How dare you! How dare you go…spying on me!'

'Spying! I haven't been spying on you! Peri told me – it seems to be common knowledge…' My voice is harsh, brittle, deep with indignation. 'But it just seems to me – it just seems that there's – a pattern…'

He's standing up. He's knocked his chair over and he's staring at me with an expression I've never seen before. He's standing up, towering up against the backdrop of storm-brewing sky, and his face is blank with anger.

In all the years I have known him, I have never experienced hostility from Yanni. Distrust from him. Yanni? I want to cry, stupidly, because it is too late, I can see that, even as I'm shaking my head –

Because I can see from his face that I have committed a crime – the crime, I realse blindingly, of showing him that the image he so carefully nurtured of himself has been shattered for me: the image, I suddenly see, which is the basis of his own belief in himself. The image, I now know, I wanted to see.

And I know also that there is no going back. But I try, nevertheless.

He's staring at me, stonily. He says nothing. And then he turns, his thongs squeaking on the soft dry sand.

I cry, 'I thought it was me, Yanni! I thought there was something I had done. But it's you – it's you. You don't want to be with anyone – you chose us all because we're not free...' But he doesn't stop – he keeps walking away. And I yell, in one last desperate shout, 'I thought it was just us, Yanni! I trusted you, Yanni! I loved you!'

He turns at last and stares at me. When he speaks his voice is thick. 'You are married. And you want to stay that way. You may not realise it yet, but you do.' His eyes have turned to grey flints. 'You made that very clear to me, that day I came to your house.'

But I wanted you to convince me otherwise, I want to cry. I wanted you to love me enough to convince me otherwise. But I can't say anything, because my voice has gone, and my eyes are burning. I cover my mouth with my hand and I try to blink away the blurriness.

And then he says one thing more. 'You know what the other problem with you is, Ven? You know the other reason why I left you? This! Exactly this! You're so intense, Ven – you take everything so seriously – you're so – so – uncool!' In the ringing silence, he stares at me. Then he turns, and is gone, disappears, masked by trees and the house.

There is a nothing. Only the wind, rising in the trees. And finally the sound of a car engine starting.

After a while, I sink from my own chair onto the sand.

I don't know how long I crouch on the sand. I cry until my breathing shudders and slows. And I become conscious of being chilled.

The sun has slipped behind a bank of cloud, and the wind off the water is brisk and cold. I stand up, shivering, and go back into the house. There's a half-finished bottle of wine on the kitchen bench. I uncork it and pour a tumbler-full, and gulp it.

I check on Sharlie. Incredibly, she's still sleeping.

And I hear a car pulling into the driveway.

What am I going to say to him? What am I going to say to him now? I think. I close my eyes. I can't see him, I think. And I can't stay here. In this house, which I thought was a house of love.

I get up. I've got to get out of here, I think. Get out, get home.

I stumble into the bedroom. I grab my case from the corner and hastily bundle in my things. I hear the front door squeak. I scramble with cosmetics, brushes. My shoes, I think, where are my shoes? I'm aware of the bedroom door swinging open but I don't look up.

'Venny.' I'm startled. I freeze.

Mark. His face like thunder.

'What – are you doing here?' My voice is faint.

He stands in the doorway. His arms are folded. His voice is clipped, quiet. 'Come to ask you the same question.'

'I...where's Ross?'

'With Julia.' He comes into the bedroom then, towards me. His face is set and grim in its mask of black beard. 'I want to know why you lied to me.'

'But how did you...' I stand still, a pair of running shoes in my hands, staring at him.

He's not listening. He glares at me. 'Why you said you were coming here to stay with Peri.'

'I – didn't lie to you.' I'm shaking my head. I breathe in, out. In, out. Calm, I think, calm, calm down. Oh, God, I think, what else can happen? 'I said I was coming over to see Peri. I didn't say I was going to stay with her.'

'So who have you been staying with?'

'I've been staying here. How did you…'

'I went to Peri's house. She told me where you were.' His voice is quietly threatening.

I shut my eyes.

I raise my head then, and look at him levelly. I know I should be honest, I know I am totally guilty of everything he suspects, but all my defences are up. My self-preservation is stronger than my conscience. There's nothing he can prove, I think. Yanni's clothes are in the bathroom – I can hide those before he sees them.

'Because of this.'

And my blood runs cold.

For out of his pocket he draws a photograph. And his voice changes. 'Is this him?'

I take it from him and stare down at Yanni's smiling, liquid-green eyes.

'IS IT?'

'Stop yelling. You'll wake Sharlie.'

'I was stripping the beds. Since you were off neglecting such things and I do like clean sheets to sleep in. It fell out of your pillowcase. Now tell me he didn't fuck you!' He finishes triumphantly with a shout even the fish in the channel must hear. That Charlotte must hear. But there's no frightened squawk. She's used to raised voices…

I stare at the photograph. For one moment I think, all right, I'll tell him the truth. I'll tell him the truth.

What truth? That I've been in love, in love all my adult life, with Yanni? That I had thought I was ready to leave Mark, to live with Yanni on this pagan island, and raise my children with Yanni here? But that it was all an illusion: Yanni didn't love me back, didn't love me back – has never loved me. Not really.

155

I shudder. I begin to shiver. In a moment, I think, I'm going to vomit.

'I took the photograph to Julia.'

'Julia wrote the note,' I whisper. 'The one you were so upset about.' My teeth are chattering, but at least I think I have right on my side in this.

He nods. 'She told me. She told me too that I was a fool. That I was driving you away from me. Too absorbed in my work. That I have probably lost you. That yes, she had seen this man. In my house, with you.' His voice is quiet now, but laced with threat.

'It's my house too.'

'In my house. While my children were there.'

So nothing changes, I think dully. His house. His children.

Wind suddenly shakes the walls. A smatter of rain gusts against the bedroom windows.

I look back at Mark. And I say, carefully, clearly, 'His name is Yanni.' We stare at each other.

And then I sweep past him abruptly. I feel suddenly wild, reckless. Let him see, I think, let him see what his attitude to me has resulted in! Somewhere I do feel guilt, I know I have to accept blame; but overriding that is my conviction that he and Yanni are equally – equally – culpable in this! And besides, I'm too emotional, too wild with a grief of which I'm hardly yet conscious, to act in any rational way.

'Come on! Let's go find him! You can ask him what's been going on! You can ask him what part he plays in my life! You can ask him if you have anything to be afraid of, any rival to battle!'

And then I abruptly pause. Rain gushes against the windows and wind shakes the house. Where is he? I think. Where is Yanni? Back at his place? Or at his shop? No. He never went inside when he was upset. Not even when it was pouring, storming, outside. There was only one place he went whenever he wanted to think, whenever he was upset.

The ocean.

'Come on,' I say to Mark. 'Let's get Charlotte and go.' My voice is calm and cold. 'I want you to meet him. It's about time. I know where he'll be. Cylinder, probably. He knew the surf was getting rough. He wouldn't risk Main. Surely.'

My waterproof coat is hanging over the back of a chair. I struggle into it. Mark's already wearing a parker.

'You get Sharlie while I pack up the rest of our stuff. Might as well go straight to the ferry after. You can warm some milk for her on the stove.'

He's staring at me and I can see he's uncertain. Confused. So I go into the bathroom and clatter the rest of our things. I shove Yanni's clothes and toothbrush into the cupboard under the sink. After a moment, I hear Mark go in to Charlotte.

We drive in silence to Cylinder Beach. Charlotte is still half asleep. Mark parks the car off the road and I stumble out into the rain and wind. It's late afternoon, and darkening. There is a heavy grey ceiling of cloud low over the sea, and swaths of gusting water shiver across its surface. I stand under a tea tree and stare out at the surf. It's big, heaving: you can see the rip sweeping all along the shallows. A wave explodes on the rocky outcrop off to the right. I can't see any surfers out there. The beach is deserted as well. Yanni's car isn't parked anywhere close.

Rain trickles down the front of my neck and the wind gusts wet against my face. What am I doing? I think. What am I trying to prove? Why don't I just give up, now, and go home?

Because I'm uneasy. I've suddenly become uneasy. Yanni was upset. As I've never seen him. He actually lost his cool. Which means he might not make rational decisions. His judgement might be out.

I go back to the car. 'Let's go to Main Beach,' I say abruptly. 'Or – maybe just check Deadman's…and Frenchman's…on the way.'

Mark is silent; his face is a mask. The rain is heavier now, and the light is fading fast. We drive slowly along Point Lookout with the headlights on. Perhaps, after all, I think suddenly, he's simply gone to the pub?

'Pull in here,' I say.

Mark presses his lips together but turns in to the hotel car park. Not too many drinkers have arrived yet, and I see at a glance that Yanni's battered station wagon is not there.

We continue along the hill. To get to Deadman's or Frenchman's Beaches, he'd have to park the car on the road's sandy verge and clamber down the cliff. The parked cars loom in the headlights. No russet-gold station wagon near Deadman's. We drive on slowly. And I see it.

'Stop!' I say. 'He's here. He'll be surfing.'

In the dim light of the car's cocoon, Mark stares at me in disbelief. But I'm not thinking about Mark now. I'm thinking about Frenchman's Beach and its rip and the wind tearing at the trees. I'm thinking about Yanni, my lover…

The wind lifts the car door from my hand and slams it with a spatter of water. I hear Mark's door creaking open, but I'm already struggling against the wind and rain to the cliff.

I stand on the brink of it. It rolls under the rain jaggedly down to the beach, bumpy with boulders and pandanus and bowed grass. There's a goat trail winding down it…a goat trail, like perhaps the goat trails Yanni tripped down in his golden youth in Greece, when he was a god, a god to everyone he touched…

I look out at the sea. At first all I see is the heavy grey rain and the dull heaving restlessness of the ocean. The waves, big, foaming, power in from far out, then break, the spray fanning up – suddenly, suddenly, I seem to see, like the profiles of charging boars, their heads lowered, the fanned hair on their humped backs for an instant framed against the darkness of the sky…

And then I glimpse, in the tumult of a crashing wave, the glint of a surfboard.

I gasp. Mark is beside me, but I'm hardly aware of him. I start down the goat track, slipping despite my rubber-soled sneakers. Mark comes after me, but I'm quick, sliding, falling, scraping my jeans and hands, tearing my waterproof jacket. I land with a thump on the hard, wet sand. I tear off my shoes, my jacket. I begin to wade into the sea. It swirls around me, dragging my feet from underneath me, soaking my jeans so they're like weights around my calves. My thighs. I stumble into a sudden hole: my head goes under. I surface, gasping at the cold.

'Yanni!' I scream. 'Yanni!'

I get a foothold, but a wave swamps me. There's a powerful rip, and it sweeps me, holds me under, and drags me out to sea obliquely. I surface gagging and spluttering. 'Yanni!'

Another wave crashes, and I see, off to my right, against the rip, the flash of the board again. I struggle towards it – and get dumped by a massive incoming set. I'm swirled into the sand; my head is thrown, knocked against the sea floor, and then ripped upward.

I surface groggily to Mark's voice, shouting, urgent: 'Venny! Ven! What the hell are you doing?'

He's off to my left, so that the current is sweeping me to him. I notice that he, sensibly, has ripped off nearly everything… And then another wave picks me up and in reflex I begin to paddle, frantically, all the stuff Yanni taught me about waves and body surfing coming back to me, magically; and somehow I ride the wave and keep it from dumping me and I crash straight into Mark. And then we're both flung in a tangle of sandy, gritty clothes, limbs and hair into the shallows.

When I get my breath back, when I can sit up and stop spitting out seawater, I raise my face to Mark. He's sprawled in the swirling, rain-pitted water, staring at me with rain running down his face and his beard. I know he's waiting for me to explain, to say something, and I open my mouth to speak –

And I see something, on the beach, to my right. I see something dark, moving, but moving dreamily, like seaweed, or some quiet, purposeless animal, off in the shallows. Withdrawing waves stream from it like wings. And out on the waves I see the glint of a surfboard again.

I struggle up. 'Come on,' I whisper, my lips clumsy with cold. 'Come with me, Mark.'

He stares up at me, his face grim. 'Where to now? What the hell are you playing at, Ven? Look at us! You could have drowned! And Charlotte's back in the car…'

'Charlotte?' I turn in sudden fear.

'She's okay. I told her to stay there, not to move…'

I look up the cliff, involuntarily. I make out the car, its dark shape against the dark sky. That's all I can see. Then I look back at the other shape on the sand.

'Come with me.' My voice is hoarse. My throat is salty and raw.

He hesitates. He frowns up at me, water swirling around and over his bare limbs… And I'm reminded suddenly, fleetingly, of that first time I swam with Yanni in this ocean, when I was eighteen and he was sixteen, and he hooted and crowed at me until I dived in, until I acknowledged him and all his beauty and charm, under the stars, under the cover of the blackness of the night and all its mystery…

And it is quite black now. Except for the white foam on the waves, visible even through the rain and darkness, washing against the dark shape, and drawing back again in feathering fans.

I'm filled with dread. I start towards it.

'Venny!' Mark stumbles to his feet.

He doesn't quite catch up to me before I get to it.

And I see what it is.

A dog.

A large, drowned dog.

20

I think sometimes love, jealousy, revenge and pain can converge into a sheer weight of anger, as debris in flowing water can converge at a single narrowing point then suddenly surge through a rift, tumbling into a formidable fall: I think the end of my relationship with Yanni, my verbal attack on him, was like that. And then, as water plateaus out to pewter as it spreads into a pool, the anger too dissipated: and in its wake was a kind of beaten panic.

Perhaps I needed my moment of terror on that beach to end it. Perhaps I needed something that seemed big, tragic, final, to end my obsession with Yanni. To dispel my illusions, once and for all: to show me that my image of Yanni was a fiction, a fantasy, concocted by my own needy heart. To anchor me at last in the still, tepid waters of reality.

Of course Yanni didn't drown. He was at the pub, after all – he'd left the car at a friend's and walked with him to the hotel. This Mark found out, when he was dressed again in his damp jeans and parka, leaving Charlotte and me in the amenities block at the Cylinder Beach caravan park, where I changed, shivering, into dry clothes. Mark asked at the pub, and the barman pointed Yanni out. But by then, because of what I told him about Yanni, Mark felt no need to approach him.

The surfboard I'd seen, an old, beaten two-fin, was later claimed by a salty veteran from Main Beach. No one claimed the dog.

I think Mark's anger was like mine, too. Built of love, jealousy, revenge and pain. I understand that. I understand that not only because I have experienced what he has, but also because it is in my nature to understand emotional reaction.

What I don't understand is Mark's, and Yanni's, inability to love with abandon. But that's perhaps because I am not wise. I am a fool…

and I see now that e.e. cummings was wrong. Kisses are not a better fate than wisdom. At least, not in my world.

I acknowledge my own culpability in this story. I acknowledge my lust, my passion, my immorality, my selfishness, my romanticism, my vanity, my ego. But I think that the other two – Mark and Yanni – are equally, in their own ways, culpable.

We have all been unfaithful, in our own fashions, to one or the other.

Life has almost returned to normal. As I write this, I'm drinking tea, on my back deck. It has been raining. The yard smells pungent: a poisonous, sappy scent I associate with noxious lantana, but which probably has nothing to do with it, since there is no lantana here. Only ferns and palms and various shrubs. When I was a child, I used to love the smell of fresh rain on earth – I used to eat the damp soil, I loved its scent so much. But the garden here doesn't smell that way.

I should do something – paint, perhaps, now the house is clean and the washing is done and Charlotte's at kindy, and Ross at school. But the Prozac makes me lethargic. I can't be bothered.

Yesterday, I received a letter from Peri. From Proserpine. She included a photograph. There she is, in a floating wedding gown, her hair wreathed with flowers and gossamer veils: her face so happy it makes me smile. And there is Aunt Dem beside her, in summer green, a silk dress the colour of sugar cane sheathing her sturdy body, and a bemused smile on her face. There is a balding man beside her with his arm around her waist. Bob, the man Peri wanted her mother to form a relationship with. I wonder if that is what has happened.

I phoned Aunt Dem eventually, when things had settled down between Mark and me. I told Mark that night on the beach, when I thought Yanni had drowned, that Yanni was my half-brother, and that I'd only found out recently. He wanted to know why I hadn't told him. I said it had been a shock. He swallowed the lie, but took his usual time to forgive me. I told Aunt Dem about Haden, about the marriage proposal and New York. She wasn't happy on the phone, but two weeks later, Peri rang me to say that her mother had sent her an engagement card. Peri sounded ecstatic.

In the photo, Haden is in a suit so dark the white carnation in his buttonhole is like a flash of light...

At least, I assume it's Haden. When I first saw the man beside Peri, I was puzzled. He didn't tower over her, didn't seem massive, as that man did who summoned me to the upper rooms of his gothic house, to grill me about Yanni. This groom seemed of no great stature, and was smiling benignly.

But it had to be Haden.

I have to stop doing that, I thought then. I have to stop...mythologising people: turning them in my head into fantastic creatures, to suit my own lust for drama, or glamour, or romance. To keep my disappointment in life at bay.

Houses from dreams belong in dreams, I tell myself. And love is for the dreamers, and children for the married.

In a minute, I'll have a bath and wash my hair. I've had it cut short, for the first time in my life, and although it's no great task to care for it any more, I still maintain the ritual of washing it in the afternoon, so I have time to condition it properly and let it dry naturally. My life is full of rituals, routines. Full.

I put out my hand to close this notebook – and notice for the first time veins rising like green eels under the shiny surface of the skin on the back of my hand.